Aerin tried to ignore the tiny feather-duster flutter along the floor of her belly.

"I'm sure you'll be a perfect gentleman."

Drake's scarred eyebrow came up again in a cynical arc. "Me? Perfect?" He gave a deep chuckle of wry amusement and added, "I hardly think so." His hooded gaze dipped to her mouth for an infinitesimal moment, the atmosphere in the office charged with a nerve-tingling energy. His gaze came back to hers, and she let out a breath she had forgotten she was holding. That was surely why she was a little light-headed, right? Not just because he was looking at her with those intensely dark eyes.

"I—I'd better get going..." Aerin scooped her bag off the floor and slung its strap over her shoulder. "I'll book the flights and get back to you with the details. The dress for the dinner is formal." She turned for the door, more flustered than she cared to admit in his alluring presence. She had never been alone with him for such a long period before. How was she going to manage the weekend?

Weddings Worth Billions

Say yes...to the wedding of your dreams!

At Happily Ever After Weddings, nothing short of perfection will do! Best friends Ruby, Harper and Aerin will not rest until they give each überrich client a wedding beyond their wildest dreams.

Still, while the trio witness true love on an almost daily basis, they have yet to experience it themselves. Will the arrival of three billionaires lead Ruby, Harper and Aerin to say "I do," too?

Read Ruby and Lucas's story in
Cinderella's Invitation to Greece

Read Harper and Jack's story in
Nine Months After That Night

Read Aerin and Drake's story in
Forbidden Until Their Snowbound Night

All available now!

Melanie Milburne

FORBIDDEN UNTIL THEIR SNOWBOUND NIGHT

HARLEQUIN®
PRESENTS™

Recycling programs for this product may not exist in your area.

ISBN-13: 978-1-335-58416-8

Forbidden Until Their Snowbound Night

Copyright © 2023 by Melanie Milburne

For questions and comments about the quality of this book, please contact us at CustomerService@Harlequin.com.

Harlequin Enterprises ULC
22 Adelaide St. West, 41st Floor
Toronto, Ontario M5H 4E3, Canada
www.Harlequin.com

Printed in U.S.A.

Melanie Milburne read her first Harlequin novel at the age of seventeen, in between studying for her final exams. After completing a master's degree in education, she decided to write a novel, and thus her career as a romance author was born. Melanie is an ambassador for the Australian Childhood Foundation and a keen dog lover and trainer. She enjoys long walks in the Tasmanian bush. In 2015 Melanie won the HOLT Medallion, a prestigious award honoring outstanding literary talent.

Books by Melanie Milburne

Harlequin Presents

The Billion-Dollar Bride Hunt

The Scandalous Campbell Sisters

Shy Innocent in the Spotlight
A Contract for His Runaway Bride

Wanted: A Billionaire

One Night on the Virgin's Terms
Breaking the Playboy's Rules
One Hot New York Night

Weddings Worth Billions

Cinderella's Invitation to Greece
Nine Months After That Night

Visit the Author Profile page
at Harlequin.com for more titles.

To Louis Jacques, my beautiful toy poodle puppy. You are only a baby, but you have already brought so much laughter and joy to us. You are a mischievous pocket rocket who is unstoppable and completely and utterly adorable. xxxx

CHAPTER ONE

AERIN SAW HIM before he saw her. Drake Cawthorn was standing on the corner of the street opposite her, checking something on his phone while he waited for the 'walk' signal at the busy London intersection near his office. She took a moment to study him in secret and a little frisson danced down her spine. Drake was head and shoulders over everyone else in the crowd, with hair as black and sleek as a raven's wing and a strong nose that looked like it might once have been broken. He was wearing a dark blue suit teamed with a crisp white business shirt that emphasised his olive-toned skin. His tie was a checked blue, but it was loosened at his neck, as if he had tugged at it impatiently at one point during the day and not bothered to readjust it. He would have ticked number one on her soulmate checklist for 'tall dark and handsome' perfectly if it weren't for his bent nose and the jagged scar that interrupted his left eyebrow.

The pedestrian signal beeped and Drake lifted his head from his phone and his eyes met Aerin's. Even though she was several metres away, as soon as that bottomless dark brown gaze meshed with hers it was like being struck by a bolt of lightning.

Every. Single. Time.

Which was why she didn't cross paths with him unless there was absolutely no choice. He was the celebrity lawyer who specialised in iron-clad prenuptial agreements she and her wedding business partners recommended to clients from time to time. But Aerin wasn't standing outside his suite of rooms hoping to see him about a business matter—she preferred to email or send a text to inform him of a client's wish to see him. This visit was personal. Embarrassingly, skin-crawlingly personal. Aerin hadn't seen him face to face in months, and normally, she liked it that way. She had turned keeping her distance from him into quite a consummate skill. She found his arrant masculinity a little too...unsettling. His hardwired cynicism too jarring to a hope-less romantic as herself. And his sardonic smile and those dark chocolate eyes a little too mocking.

Drake strode across the intersection in long easy strides, carving his way through the bustle of people until he came to her side of the street. Her feet were suddenly glued to the footpath, her heart doing a compli-cated gymnastics routine in her chest and her cheeks feeling hot enough to buckle the bitumen.

'Hi there, Goldilocks. Were you on your way to see me?' His tone was as gently teas-ing as his smile.

Aerin could hardly deny it was him she had come to see when she was standing out-side his office building, but she would have dearly liked to. She had done a walk-by or two to summon up the courage to see him, oscillating whether she should go ahead or melt back in the crowd before she made a complete and utter fool of herself. But she only had five days to find a stand-in date for her high school reunion. If she didn't find a date to accompany her she would have to suffer the embarrassment of being the last of her school friends to find a partner.

Every year that passed, she was becoming more and more of a pariah to her friends. The only singleton. The only virgin. The pitying looks from her school friends were worse each year, she was sure she wasn't imagining it. The covert whispers, the speculation about her single status, the pointed questions and glances at her ringless left hand, when each of her friends had such gorgeous sparklers winking on their ring fingers you could practically see them from outer space. It was making her wonder if her dream of finding her own Mr Perfect was a little…well, out of touch with reality. It was quite hard to meet people these days and she wasn't going to download the social media app unless things got desperate. Well, even more desperate than they already were with her nearly thirty and never been kissed.

But she *believed* in true love.

It was her goal, her lifelong hope.

Her Mr Perfect Soulmate had to be out there. All she had to do was find him.

Aerin gave Drake a mock glower. 'I wish you'd stop calling me that.'

His wide grin made his eyes dance and fine lines crinkle at the corners. 'I've been calling you that since you had braces on your teeth and pimples on your chin. I must say, you've improved greatly with age.'

As her older brother's friend from university, Drake had been a regular visitor to her family home in years past. For years he had simply been Tom's friend, Drake Cawthorn, barely worthy of her notice. But once she hit late puberty, she became increasingly aware of him as any young woman did over a handsome and charming man. Fortunately, she had never embarrassed herself by communicating any interest in him. Not that a worldly playboy like him would ever be interested in someone as homespun and conservative as her.

'Please don't remind me I'm turning thirty in January.'

Drake widened his eyes as if in stunned surprise. 'No way. Got anything planned? A big party to celebrate?'

Aerin could feel a blush stealing over her cheeks hot enough to contribute to global warming. What was there to celebrate about turning thirty when she didn't have a partner, had never had a partner and had not even been kissed? Argh. Her dream of finding Mr Perfect before she turned the big Three O was becoming a nightmare and her biological clock was ticking loud enough to wake up an entire cemetery of bodies. She shifted her gaze from his and gave a dismissive shrug. 'I'm not sure. Maybe.'

He jerked his head in the direction of his suite of rooms. 'Did you want to see me about a client? I've got just under an hour before I'm due in court.'

Aerin shifted her weight from foot to foot and readjusted her tote-bag strap over her left shoulder, conscious of his steady gaze. 'Erm… I don't want to bother you when you're busy…'

'I've always got time for you. Besides, you send a lot of business my way.' His eyes twinkled again, and he added, 'I heard your other business partner, Harper, got herself engaged to Jack Livingstone. Are they going to come and see me about a prenup?'

'Not that I know of.'

'Pity. With Jack's sort of wealth, it could be a messy divorce without one.'

Aerin gave a stiff smile to cover her annoyance at his cynicism. 'I don't think they're ever going to divorce. They're too much in love and besides, they have baby Marli to consider.'

Drake shrugged one impossibly broad shoulder. 'Everyone is in love until they aren't.'

'Have you ever been in love?' The question popped out of her mouth before she could slam the emergency brakes on her tongue.

'No. How about you?'

Her cheeks warmed up again and she couldn't hold his gaze. A relationships cynic like Drake would mock her quest to find the love of her life. But it was no secret she was waiting not just for Mr Right but Mr Perfect. 'No, but I'd like to one day.'

There was a short but weighted silence, even the sounds of rushing pedestrians and busy traffic seeming to fade into the background.

'What did you want to see me about?' Drake asked, looking down at her with a small frown between his eyebrows.

Aerin chewed at one side of her lower lip. 'It doesn't matter.' She began to step away, but he reached out and placed his broad-spanned and tanned hand on her forearm. Her cashmere coat wasn't enough of a barrier to block the electric heat of his touch. She could not think of a time when he had ever touched her before—or at least not since he had teasingly ruffled her hair when she was a kid. Her gaze connected to his and another fizz of awareness shot through her.

His hand fell away from her arm as if he too had felt the same current of energy, his frown deepening above his dark brown eyes. 'Is everything all right?' His voice was pitched low, a deep rough burr of sound that sent another delicate shiver along her spine.

Aerin swallowed thickly and gave him a strained smile. 'Can we take this somewhere a little more private?'

'Sure.'

He led the way to the front of his office building and Aerin followed, wondering if she was being a fool for even contemplating asking him to be a stand-in date for her reunion. But who else could she ask? She didn't want to take a stranger or someone off a dating app. She needed someone who could act convincingly as her love interest for the weekend meet-up in Scotland. Drake was the most experienced man she knew and, even better, he had known her for years. He was perfect…well, not exactly perfect according to her soulmate checklist but good enough to get her over the line. She could not suffer the embarrassment of being the only single person at her school reunion weekend—their last reunion before one of the girls emigrated to Australia with her husband. If Aerin didn't show up, they would assume it was because of her feelings about still being alone. She had to go and she had to take a stand-in partner. That was the plan.

'My office is on the top floor,' Drake said, walking past the four lifts situated on one side of the marble-floored foyer.

Aerin gave him a sideways glance of horror. 'You're not expecting me to walk up fifty flights of stairs?'

His mouth tilted in one of his wry smiles that never failed to make her stomach flip-flop. 'I have my own private lift back here.' He shouldered open a door and indicated for her to come through while he held it open for her. She moved past him in the doorway, catching an alluring waft of his lemon-and-lime-based aftershave on her way past his tall and lean athletic frame. The door closed behind him with a solid thump, and he led her to a lift marked Private. Drake took out a security tag from his trouser pocket and used it against the sensor and the doors swished open. He held one muscular arm against the lift door and said, 'After you.'

Aerin stepped inside the lift and he followed her in, the doors closing on a whisper behind him. The sensation of being enclosed in a small space alone with Drake Cawthorn sent her heart rate soaring. The lift was mirrored on three sides, and she caught a glimpse of her flushed features and inwardly cringed. Why did she always have to act like an awkward teenage girl around him? Was it because he was the epitome of sophisticated man about town? A self-made billionaire playboy who had women from all over the globe flocking after him? She was a successful businesswoman, not a gauche teenager.

Well…a single-and-hating-it successful businesswoman. She loved the success, not the singledom.

There was a pinging sound when the lift arrived at Drake's floor. 'This way,' he said, and she followed him down a wide plushily carpeted corridor, past a reception area where a middle-aged woman was typing on a computer. Aerin was fairly certain it was the same woman she had spoken to on a couple of occasions when she'd called to book an appointment for clients.

'Hold my calls, please, Cathleen,' Drake said.

Cathleen's smile of greeting was friendly towards her but Aerin wasn't sure if it was one of recognition or not. 'Will do.'

Drake led Aerin to a door marked with his name on a simple plaque. He opened the door and gave a brief on-off smile to indicate for her to go in. She stepped over the threshold and glanced around at the neat but understated décor. Drake's qualifications were framed on one wall to the left of his large wooden desk. She suspected they were only there to display to his clients he was more than qualified to act for them rather than out of any sense of pride in his own achievements. She knew that Drake had graduated with First Class Honours and taken out the university prize, but she had heard that from her brother, not Drake. There was a selection of artwork on the other walls—nothing too over the top but tasteful landscapes in an old-world style—and the windows afforded a spectacular view over the River Thames and Tower Bridge.

'Take a seat. Can I get Cathleen to bring you a coffee or tea?' Drake asked, shrugging off his coat and hanging it inside a cupboard near his desk.

'No, thanks. I had one not long ago.' Actually, she'd had three, which was probably why her pulse was racing so fast. Caffeine courage instead of Dutch courage was never a good idea. Her heart was palpitating from the stimulant…or was it because the thought of asking Drake Cawthorn this favour was sending her heart rhythm way out of whack?

Aerin sat, knowing he was too polite to take his own seat until she had taken hers. She placed her tote bag on her lap and laid her hands on top to keep it from slipping to the floor.

Drake sat in his office chair and rolled it closer to his desk, his forearms resting on the polished surface, his fingers loosely interlaced. Aerin's gaze drifted to those long, tanned fingers and she wondered what it would feel like to have them glide along her skin. She tried to disguise a little shiver, tried but failed. Why was she suddenly thinking about his hands touching her? He was not the type of man she could ever build a future with. He was too worldly, too cynical.

'Are you cold? I can turn up the heating if you like.'

'No, I'm fine...' She licked her lips and forced a smile, conscious of the glowing warmth in her cheeks and the nerves eating at the lining of her stomach like piranha teeth. 'I have a...a favour to ask.'

He lifted his scar-interrupted eyebrow in an arc, his sharply intelligent gaze unwavering on hers. 'Go on.'

Aerin gripped her tote bag a little more firmly. Her heart beat out a syncopated rhythm in her chest. *Boom-pitty-boom... pitty-pitty-boom-boom.*

'I have a high school reunion this weekend. It's a drinks and dinner catch-up in a remote village an hour out of Edinburgh, close to our old boarding school, and I... I have no one to take me.'

Drake lifted his arms off his desk and leaned back in his chair, his expression unreadable. 'Why can't you go on your own?'

Another wave of heat exploded in her cheeks. 'For the last twelve years I've met up with my school friends once a year just before Christmas and I've always gone alone. It wasn't so bad in the early years because some of the girls were single or between partners. But I'm now the only one without a partner. I can't face yet another year without producing a date. It's so mortifying to be the last singleton. I'll never hear the end of it. They teased me so much last time I thought I would die of embarrassment.'

'Then why go if they're only going to give you a hard time?'

Aerin absently fiddled with the silver buckle on her tote bag. His gaze flicked to her busy fingers and she forced herself to stop their restive movements. She got the sense he was reading her, analysing her, observing every nuance of her expression and it made her feel exposed and terribly unsophisticated. He was only seven years older than her but in terms of experience it was more like a century. An aeon.

'We have a perfect track record of meeting up. Twelve years and not one of us has failed to show up. I don't want to be the one to break it. But if I were not to show up, everyone is going to assume I'm embarrassed about still being single, so I have to show up with someone—I can't win either way. I was talking to Harper and she suggested I ask you, since you've known me a long time. It's either that or hire a male escort.'

Drake shot out of his chair, his features set in frowning lines. 'You will *not* do that.' The stern note of authority in his tone would have annoyed her on any other occasion but for some strange reason, this time, it did not.

She looked up at him hopefully. 'So, does that mean you'll be my date for the night?'

Drake ran a hand over his face and then loosened his tie even further. His frown was more of a scowl and his mouth was set in a firm line. 'I thought you said it was a weekend thing?'

'It is but I would only need you to be there for the drinks and dinner thing on the Friday night. I'll tell them you had to fly back for work or something.'

He continued to hold her gaze with unwavering intensity. 'So, what's the story you're going to spin to them about our... relationship?'

'I'll tell them we've fallen madly in love and—'

He held up his right hand like a stop sign and his features screwed up in distaste. 'Whoa there, Goldilocks. No offence but I'm not the type of guy to fall head over heels in love. Why can't we say we're having a fling?'

Aerin shifted her lips from side to side. 'Because I'm not the type of girl to have a fling.'

'You must have had plenty of flings, you're almost thirty.'

There was a silence so intense Aerin could hear the creak of her chair when she shifted position. She slowly lifted her gaze to his and saw the dawning shock and surprise.

'Are you telling me you're a *virgin*?'

The word seemed to bounce off the four walls of the room. Did he have to make it sound so...so shocking? Plenty of people were celibate for various reasons. Aerin let her bag slip to the floor as she stood. 'I know it's a little unusual but that's why I need a date this weekend. I've been teased about my virginal status for years.'

'Is there some reason you haven't…?'

'Done the deed?' Aerin sighed. 'Yes. I'm waiting for my soulmate to show up. I don't want to waste myself on someone who doesn't get the importance of what this means to me. I want everything about my first time to be perfect.'

Drake walked over to the windows of his office, and, placing his hands on his lean hips, looked out at the view below. She hadn't noticed before how broad his back and shoulders were from behind. They tapered down to trim hips and a taut bottom and long lean legs. Her mind began to undress him and her heart rate picked up again. She could imagine he would look wonderfully sexy in nothing but his olive-toned skin. What would it feel like to run her hands over his naked flesh? She was shocked at her wayward thoughts, wondering why they were entering her mind now. She was only interested in him as a stand-in date, not as a real date.

It was a moment or two before Drake turned around to look at her, his hands going back down by his sides. The afternoon sun coming in from behind him cast his features into shadow, giving him an even more rakish look.

'Look, I'm flattered you asked me, but—'

'Please don't say no, Drake. I'm desperate. I can't go alone, not this year because it's the last year we will all be together because one of the girls is moving to Australia with her husband.' Aerin didn't care that she was at the begging stage. 'We don't have to mention it to anyone. Even Tom doesn't have to know or my parents. In fact, it's probably best if they don't hear about it.'

Drake moved back behind his desk but didn't sit in his chair. He stood grasping the back of it instead, his fingers white-knuckled against the leather. 'Will the press be there?'

'No, it's a private event.'

'But no doubt you and your friends will post photos on social media.'

Aerin tried not to think of how many followers some of her so-called influencer friends had. At last count it was in the hundreds of thousands. 'I'll tell them not to post any photos of us. I'll tell them we're keeping our relationship a secret from my family for a little while longer. I'm sure they'll go along with it. They know how full-on my dad can be.'

Drake let out a long sigh and removed his hands from the back of his chair. 'I'm not sure I'm the right guy for the job.' He shook his head as if he still couldn't believe she had asked him. 'It's got all sorts of wrong about it.'

Disappointment swept through her and she caught her lip between her teeth. 'It's just one night. You don't have to do anything but pretend to be my partner. I'm not asking you to actually *be* my partner.'

'I'm not planning on being anyone's partner.'

Drake resumed his seat but didn't roll the chair close to the desk, sitting with one leg casually crossed over his other knee, the fingers of his right hand lightly drumming against his thigh. His eyes didn't leave hers and she fought against the desire to squirm in her seat. He had his lawyer face on, the stillness of his features revealing nothing of the razor-sharp inner workings of his mind.

'Because you're afraid to love someone in case they hurt you?' she ventured.

His fingers stopped drumming against his leg and there was a sudden movement in the back of his gaze—a movement as quick as a camera shutter click. But then his lips twisted in a sardonic smile. 'People can hurt you whether you love them or not.'

'I guess…'

He uncrossed his leg and rolled the chair back to the desk. 'Okay. I'll do it. But only because I don't want you to get in over your head with someone who might do the wrong thing by you.'

Aerin breathed out a gusty sigh of relief. 'Oh, thank you so much. I was working myself into such a state at the thought of hiring someone or taking a stranger and having to share a room with them.'

There was a long beat of silence.

'Will you be comfortable sharing a room with me?' His tone was mildly teasing, the glint in his eyes even more so.

Aerin tried to ignore the tiny feather-duster flutter along the floor of her belly. Tried to ignore the sudden leap of her pulse and the hitch of her breath in her throat. 'I'm sure you'll be a perfect gentleman.'

His scarred eyebrow came up again in a cynical arc. 'Me? Perfect?' He gave a deep chuckle of wry amusement and added, 'I hardly think so.' His hooded gaze dipped to her mouth for an infinitesimal moment, the atmosphere in the office charged with a nerve-tingling energy. His gaze came back to hers, and she let out a breath she had forgotten she was holding. That was surely why she was a little light-headed, right? Not just because he looked at her with those intensely dark eyes.

'I—I'd better get going…' Aerin scooped up her bag off the floor and slung its strap over her shoulder. 'I'll book the flights and get back to you with the details. The dress for the dinner is formal. I know that seems a little over the top, but we've always done it that way.' She turned for the door, more flustered than she cared to admit in his alluring presence. She had never been alone with him for such a long period before. How was she going to manage the weekend?

'Aerin.' His deep voice stopped her in her tracks. He had called her Goldilocks for years; she couldn't remember the last time she had heard her name on his lips.

She turned to look at him, clutching her tote bag close to her side. 'Yes?'

His dark eyes held hers for a heart-stopping moment, his expression unusually sombre. 'You'll be safe with me. You have my word.'

'Thank you.' She gave him a quick smile and turned again for the door.

'Another thing—I'll book the flights.'

'But I don't expect you to pay—'

'It's not a problem.'

Aerin knew it would be pointless arguing with him. 'Okay, that's kind of you, thank you.'

'Wait. I'll come down with you.' He picked up a folder of papers off his desk and slid them into a leather briefcase, then closed the lid and locked it. He took his jacket out of the cupboard and shrugged himself back into it. Then he lifted his hand to his tie and tightened it back in place close to his neck. The actions were things she had seen her brother and father do hundreds if not thousands of times and yet, when Drake did them, there was something so...so arrantly masculine and so darn sexy about it.

They travelled down in the private lift in a silence that throbbed with something Aerin had not been aware of before. She cast covert glances at him, but his features were set in inscrutable lines. The lift doors whooshed open on the ground floor and she stepped out. She was aware of his tall frame only a step or two behind her, aware of the citrus scent of his aftershave, and aware of her body's secret reaction to him.

Aerin turned to say goodbye. 'Thank you again. I hope you didn't have anything important planned for this weekend?'

His smile was lopsided and didn't reach his eyes. 'Nothing I couldn't cancel at short notice.'

'Erm... I didn't think to ask but are you currently seeing anyone? I mean, that could make things rather awkward, and I would hate to complicate things for—'

'No.' His answer was unmistakably definitive.

'Oh, I thought you nearly always had someone on the go.'

'Not this close to Christmas.'

Aerin frowned. 'But Christmas is a month away. I thought you changed partners just about every week.'

A shutter came down over his face. 'I've got to rush. I have a mediation meeting at court in ten minutes. See you Friday.' He turned to leave.

'Drake?'

He stopped moving to look down at her. 'Yes?'

Aerin gave him a tremulous smile. 'You won't suddenly change your mind and leave me to face the violins alone?'

He gave a quizzical frown. 'The violins?'

'It's a saying Harper used. It refers to the pity symphony I get every year from my school friends for still being single.'

His frown faded and his mouth tilted in a half-smile. 'I won't change my mind.'

Change his mind? That was exactly what Drake knew he should do and yet he couldn't bring himself to let Aerin down. But what the freaking hell was he doing agreeing to partner his best friend's kid sister to a re-union in Scotland? A weekend pretending to be someone he was not. He was not Prince

Charming or Mr Perfect or Mr Right or Mr Soulmate. But how could he let innocent and naïve Aerin take anyone else? She was as trusting and idealistic as he was cynical and jaded. Her confession about still being a virgin had shocked him to the backbone and beyond. He knew she was conservative but not to the point that she had left it so long to experience sex.

Of course he had to agree to take her to the reunion. What other option was there? How could he be sure some other less principled guy wouldn't jump at the chance to take her virginity as some sort of prize? The most Drake had ever done with her was ruffle her golden hair as a kid. But placing his hand on her arm earlier had sounded a warning in his body. A warning that she was not a gangly teenager any more. She was an adult woman with gentle feminine curves and a soft pillowy mouth he could barely take his eyes off. A mouth he could not stop thinking about tasting to see if it was as sweet and delicious as it looked.

He had never really noticed her before other than as his friend's younger sister. But sitting opposite her in his office, watching her drum up the courage to ask him to help her, had shifted something in their relationship. A subtle shift that made him aware of her in ways he had not been before—or at least not consciously. Aerin was not supermodel-gorgeous, but she had a girl-next-door natural beauty that was equally breathsnatching. Her golden hair was straight and fell past her shoulders to the middle of her back in a silken skein. Her body was as slim and finely boned as a ballerina's, her eyes a smoky grey-blue. Her ski-slope nose was—unlike his—perfectly aligned above a full-lipped Cupid's bow mouth. A mouth that promised sweetness and sensuality in its plump curves. A mouth that was forbidden territory for someone like him.

He could look but not touch and not taste. That would be crossing a line he had sworn he would never cross. He wasn't interested in complicating his life with a young woman who had fairy dust in her eyes. Aerin was after perfection in a partner, she believed in for ever love and had waited this long to find it. Thirty years old and still a virgin? How could that be possible in this day and age?

He had lost his virginity the month after

losing his family. Back then, sex had been a mind-numbing escape from pain and in a way it still was. He never allowed himself to get close to anyone other than physically. His relationships were transactional and brief. No promises, no strings, no emotions other than lust, which wasn't an emotion in his opinion but a physical drive. He dealt with it efficiently and, of course, respectfully and always consensually but that was as far as it ever went. He had sworn off ever falling in love and did everything in his power to keep the armour around his heart in place. Armour so thick and strong and such a part of him now, he was barely aware of it being there.

But sweet untouched and innocent Aerin with her heart-shaped face and kissable mouth was a threat because he already had a relationship with her of sorts. A hard to define relationship but it was long-lasting, and he didn't want to compromise it or his relationship with her brother, Tom, and his parents, who he also considered friends. Too many people would get hurt if he didn't keep the boundary lines in place. And the last thing he wanted was to hurt anyone, especially people he cared about. He had paid a high price for relaxing his guard when he was fifteen.

He would *not* do it again.

Aerin Drysdale was off limits to him in every way. Too sweet, too innocent, too good for a man who had such dark secrets in his past.

CHAPTER TWO

AERIN HAD A work meeting the following day with her business partners, Ruby and Harper. Ruby was only just back from a brief honeymoon having got married to Lucas Rothwell a couple of weeks ago. And Harper had recently become engaged to Jack Livingstone, the father of her surprise baby, Marli. Witnessing her friends' blissful happiness only made Aerin's single status all the more painful. Day in day out, she was surrounded by happy couples; her parents were as in love after thirty-seven years of marriage as they were when they first got together. Her brother Tom and his wife, Saskia, had been married six years and, although they were struggling with some fertility issues, she knew they were a match made in heaven and would stay together for ever.

Aerin believed in true love and desperately wanted it for herself. She had planned her future since she was a little kid. She was meant to be married with two kids by now. No way did she ever think she would still be a virgin so close to turning thirty but there hadn't been anyone she was even mildly attracted to…until now.

But she *wasn't* going to think about Drake Cawthorn as a potential partner. He was a stand-in date, that was all.

'So, did you ask him?' Harper asked with a teasing waggle of her eyebrows.

'Ask who?' Ruby said, having a turn at cuddling baby Marli, who was soundly asleep.

'I told Aerin to ask Drake Cawthorn to be her stand-in date for her reunion weekend,' Harper explained to Ruby, then, turning back to Aerin, asked, 'So, did you ask him?'

'I did.'

'And?' Both Harper and Ruby said in unison and with almost identical expectant expressions.

Aerin leaned forward to put her electronic planner on the table in front of her. 'It took some work, but he finally agreed.'

'Oh, wow,' Ruby said, eyes gleaming with excitement. 'This could be the start of something.'

Aerin rolled her eyes in an expressive manner. 'I don't think so. Drake might be handsome in a rugged way, but he doesn't tick any of my other boxes.' There was a part of her that was starting to wonder if there was anyone out there who could tick all her boxes, but she didn't want to admit it to her friends. She barely wanted to admit it to herself. She had clung to the hope of finding a perfect partner so ardently and passionately for so long, it would make her look foolish to back down now. Surely the right man was out there for her? How could she lose faith now?

'How well do you know him?' Ruby asked. 'I knew Lucas since I was a child and yet I didn't truly get to know him until he whisked me away to his private Greek island.' She gave a blissful sigh as if just thinking about that trip brought back a host of wonderful memories.

'I know him well enough to know he's not the settling down type,' Aerin said. 'My brother had enough of a job convincing him to be his best man. Weddings bring him out in a rash.'

'I guess handling all those messy divorces would make anyone in his line of work pretty cynical about relationships,' Harper said. 'Oh, well, at least you don't have to suffer the pitying looks from your school friends now. An experienced man like him is sure to do a good job of pretending to be your love interest.'

'But how are you going to convince your friends he's the real deal?' Ruby asked. 'I mean, are you going to kiss and hold hands and stuff and act all lovey-dovey?'

Aerin could feel her cheeks heating up enough to warm the room. The entire planet. 'We haven't actually discussed that angle yet. I guess we'll sort that out on the flight to Edinburgh.'

'And will you be sharing a room?' Harper asked with another waggle of her eyebrows.

'We'll have to otherwise no one is going to be convinced we're together,' Aerin said.

'I guess you could say you're waiting until you get married,' Ruby offered.

Harper gave a wry laugh. 'We're talking about Drake Cawthorn here. Who's going to believe a worldly playboy like him would wait to sleep with his intended bride? Or even that he'd propose marriage to someone in the first place?'

'Good point,' Ruby said. 'But miracles do happen. Look at us two. I didn't dare hope I could be as happy as this. Lucas is everything I could have wished for in a husband.'

'Jack is too,' Harper said with a dreamy sigh. 'We want the same for you, Aerin. It would be so wonderful to see you settled with the man of your dreams.'

Aerin wanted it too, so badly it was an ache in her heart. But Drake Cawthorn was hardly the man of her dreams. He was the complete opposite of what she wanted. She wanted someone loving and romantic, someone who believed in marriage and commitment and for ever love. Not a hardened cynic who thought marriages should only be conducted between two people with a get-out clause in place.

Drake handed his middle-aged secretary, Cathleen, some files to put away on the way out of his office on Friday after lunch.

'You're leaving early,' Cathleen said, looking up from her computer. 'Have you got something special planned for the weekend?'

'No.' He wasn't comfortable lying to his secretary, nor was he comfortable calling a weekend away in Scotland with Aerin Drysdale a special event. Even though it was. Big time. He had never been alone with her before, or at least not for that length of time. But he was confident he could keep the boundaries in place. He had drawn a line in his head and he was not stepping over it. He couldn't.

Cathleen cocked her head at him, her whisky-brown eyes curious. 'This early mark hasn't got anything to do with Aerin Drysdale's visit the other day, has it?'

Drake's eyebrows snapped together. 'You recognised her?'

Cathleen smiled. 'But of course. She planned my niece's wedding last year. She did an amazing job of it too. Gillian hardly had to do a thing but show up on time at the church. I hadn't met Aerin in person, but I recognised her from Gillian's photos. I've spoken to her on the phone a couple of times when she's booked an appointment for a client with you. She's beautiful in a rather understated way, isn't she?'

He gave a non-committal grunt. 'Passable, I suppose.'

The last thing he wanted to think about was how naturally beautiful Aerin Drysdale was. He had no interest in compromising his relationship with her older brother by having a dalliance with her. It was an unspoken bro code, and he was going to do everything in his power to hold to it. Besides, he didn't do virgins or get involved with women who wanted the fairy tale.

Cathleen's eyes danced and her smile widened. 'You've known her a long time, right? Weren't you best man at her brother's wedding a few years ago?'

'That was the first and last time I'll be standing at an altar,' Drake said with heavy conviction. 'You and I both know how often supposedly happy couples end up here a few years later hating their exes and wanting out one way or the other.'

Cathleen's shoulders went down on a sigh. 'But some couples do make it and that's what everyone wants really, isn't it? To love and be loved for the rest of their life.'

Drake had witnessed 'love' in various guises as a child. Obsessive love. Possessive love. Abusive love. Love that taunted and tortured and destroyed those to whom it was directed. But there was no way he would ever reveal the dark shadows of his childhood to his secretary or anyone else for that matter. Even his closest friend, Tom Drysdale, didn't know the ugly truth about his background. He didn't want to fall passionately in love as his parents had. He resisted it, rejected it, spurned it as if it were a deadly disease.

For in his family of origin, that was exactly what it had turned out to be—deadly.

Aerin had arranged via text message to meet Drake at the airport, but he texted back that he would pick her up himself at her flat. He had never been to her home before, only to her family's residence in Buckinghamshire. She sent him her address and waited for him to arrive with her stomach twitching with sudden nerves.

She was effectively lying to her school friends about her 'relationship' with Drake. She wasn't the most convincing liar on the planet but what else could she do now? She had already told them she was bringing her new partner. The excitement her announcement elicited on the group chat was off the charts. The fact that she had insisted on them keeping it a secret had only fuelled their interest and delight. It was too late to back out now, she had to go through with it no matter what. But every time she thought of Drake her body shivered and her heart raced. Had she made a mistake in asking him rather than a stranger?

Aerin paced the sitting room floor as the time for Drake to arrive approached, her hands twisting in front of her body.

You are spending the weekend with Drake Cawthorn.

Her pulse began to pick up its pace, her palms moistening in panic. What if she wasn't able to pull off the charade? What if she ended up being exposed as a liar and a fraud?

There was a soft knock on the door and she opened it with an overly bright smile on her face. But it wasn't Drake standing there but her elderly Scottish neighbour, Mr McPhee, who lived opposite. His equally elderly dog, Mutley, was at his feet, wagging his shaggy tail from side to side and looked up at her through rheumy eyes not unlike his owner's. Mutley had probably been adorably cute in puppyhood but as a senior he had developed some bald patches on his rough coat. He was of indiscriminate breeding and short and stout with stumpy legs and with a black patch over one eye like a pirate. One of his ears pointed up, the other folded down and his jaw was out of line, the bottom overshot like a drawer that hadn't been closed properly. Oh, and he had terrible breath and farted. A lot.

'Oh, hello, Mr McPhee. Hi, Mutley. I'm just heading out for the weekend. Did you want me for something?'

'Sorry to bother you, lass, but do you have a wee cup of sugar? I seem to have run out.' Mr McPhee's expression was sheepish and Aerin knew from experience he didn't need the sugar as much as he needed human contact. Widowed eight years ago, he was close to ninety and had no relatives living nearby, or at least, none who visited regularly. He often popped over for a cup of tea and a chat and she enjoyed his company for he reminded her of her maternal grandfather, who was also a proud Scot.

'Of course. Do you want to come in while I get it? I have some of those treats Mutley likes so much.'

'I don't want to take up your time. Where are you off to for the weekend?'

'Erm… Scotland, actually.'

Mr McPhee shuffled into her flat with Mutley waddling beside him. 'Och, now then, that will be good for you, although November's not the best time. Cold and grey and wet. You might even get a flurry of snow. It wouldn't be the first time.'

'I know but it's a high school reunion, so we'll be inside most of the time.' Aerin bent down to give Mutley a doggy treat, and then went to her small pantry for the sugar.

There was another knock on the door, firmer this time and her heart gave a skip. 'Erm, will you excuse me for a moment? That's my lift here to collect me.'

Aerin went to the front door and opened it to find Drake standing there dressed casually for travelling in jeans and a roll-neck cashmere sweater and a black, butter-soft leather jacket. She gave him a nervous smile.

'I'm just helping my neighbour with something. I won't be long.'

Just then, Mr McPhee shuffled out of the kitchen with Mutley close behind, the dog's long claws click-clacking on the polished floorboards until he got to the carpet runner. 'Is this your beau, lass? About time, I say.' Mr McPhee thrust out his hand to Drake. 'Hamish McPhee.'

Drake grasped the older man's hand. 'Drake Cawthorn. Pleased to meet you, Mr McPhee.'

Aerin was conscious of the heat pooling in her cheeks, which did not bode well for the weekend charade. Or global warming. She would have to get used to people calling Drake her beau or boyfriend or…or lover. Gulp.

Mutley sniffed Drake's leather shoes and looked up at him and gave a croaky bark, his tail wagging. At first, Aerin thought Drake was going to ignore the dog but after a moment, he bent down and gave Mutley a gentle scratch behind the ears. Something passed over Drake's features—a flattening of his mouth, a tightening of his jaw, a rapid blink of his eyes. Then he straightened and glanced at her. 'There's no rush if you want to chat to Mr McPhee. I'll take your luggage down to the car.'

'Och, no, I'm going home anyway for it's time for this wee chap's supper,' Mr McPhee said, whistling to Mutley to follow him. 'Have a grand time, you two. I wish I was your age again. It's times like these I miss my Maisie. But we had sixty-one years together, so I should be grateful, eh?'

'That's a lovely attitude to have, Mr McPhee,' Aerin said. 'But it must still be terribly hard for you.'

'Aye, lass, it is, but that's what you sign up for when you love someone. If you're lucky you grow old together but then one day they're no longer with you and all you have are the memories.'

'It was nice to meet you, Mr McPhee,' Drake said, and extended his hand again.

The old man shook it warmly. 'Take good care of her, eh? She's one in a million.'

'I will.'

A short time later, Aerin was sitting in Drake's showroom-perfect sports car, her luggage stowed in the boot along with his.

'Mr McPhee is rather a sweetheart,' she said to fill the silence. 'I hope it didn't embarrass you when he mistook you for my…erm…'

Drake sent her a sideways glance, his dark eyes glinting. 'Lover?'

Another wave of heat flooded her cheeks. 'I actually told him you were my lift to the airport, but he jumped to conclusions.'

'Why haven't you dated anyone?'

Aerin looked at her hands rather than meet his gaze. 'I don't want to make a mistake. Choosing your life partner is such an important decision. Your entire life can be shifted way off course if you get it wrong. I want to get it right the first time. I don't want to have a trail of broken relationships behind me. I've had good role-modelling from my parents and grandparents of how a well-functioning relationship works, so I don't want to waste time on dating men who don't come close to my dream partner, my perfect soulmate.'

Drake started the engine with a throaty rumble and put the car in gear. 'Is there such a thing?' he asked with a note of cynicism in his tone.

'A perfect soulmate? Of course there is.

Look at my parents. They're still madly in love all these years down the track. And then there's Tom. He and Saskia are so perfect for each other in every way.'

A frown brought his dark brows closer together. 'You think so?'

Aerin glanced at him with a frown. 'Of course I do. I know things are a little tough on them now after Saskia's last miscarriage but Tom adores her and she adores him.'

He didn't respond other than give a non-committal grunt.

There was a lengthy silence broken only by the swish of the tyres on the wet roads on the way to the airport.

'Drake? There's something we need to discuss before we get to the reunion.' Aerin took a deep breath and continued, 'If we're going to convince everyone we're a couple, we have to act like we're in love.'

'How do you know a couple is in love? What signs do you look for?'

Aerin immediately pictured Ruby and Lucas and Harper and Jack in her mind. 'Well, they usually touch each other a lot, hold hands or have their arms around each other.'

'So, you'd be okay with me doing that with you?'

'I guess…' Aerin shivered at the thought of his muscled arms around her. He had a tall and rangy build with muscles taut and toned by endurance exercise. What would it feel like to have those arms gather her close? To have her chest pressed against the rock wall of his? To be so physically close she would feel the hard contours of his body against her softer ones? She had never been that close to a man.

'What about kissing?'

Her heart skipped a beat. 'What about it?'

'Is that something you'd expect an in-love couple to do?'

Aerin licked her suddenly dry lips. 'Yes, but not all couples are comfortable with public displays of affection.'

'So, no passionate kissing in public, then.'

Aerin twisted her hands together in her lap, suddenly imagining Drake's firm lips pressed to hers. What would he taste like? What would it feel like to have his mouth against hers in a passionate kiss? She had never been game enough to allow anyone to kiss her. She had always wanted her first kiss to be perfect, but she had spent so much time planning it, it hadn't happened.

'I guess a peck on the cheek or a brief kiss on the lips might be okay...'

'Anything else I should do to be convincing?'

'Well, one thing I've noticed about men who are in love with their partners and vice versa is a certain look they have in their eyes, kind of soft and tender and dewy.'

Drake screwed up his face in a grimace. 'That's probably outside my acting capabilities, I'm afraid. I'm not the soppy type.'

'Yet another fail on my checklist,' Aerin said not quite under her breath.

She felt rather than saw his glance. 'Tell me about this checklist of yours. I probably should know what's on it if I'm supposed to be pretending to be the man who's actually managed to tick every box. How many are there?'

'Eight.'

He whistled through his teeth. 'I'm starting to see why you've got to almost thirty without finding a partner.'

Aerin flashed him an irritated look. 'Personally, I think there would be a lot less divorces if men and women did think a little more deeply about what they want in a life partner. It would save a lot of heartache in the end.'

'I'm sure it would.' Something about his tone brought her gaze back to his but his expression was unreadable. 'What's number one on your list?' he said after a moment's silence.

'I'm only going to tell you if you promise not to mock me.'

'Okay, I promise not to mock you.'

She studied his inscrutable features for a beat or two. 'I know it's a bit clichéd, but I want a man who is tall and dark and handsome.'

'Why not a blond or red-haired man?'

'I can't explain it other than I've always seen myself with someone with dark hair.'

'And number two?'

'Well, this is one you certainly don't meet. I want a man who believes in love and is a romantic at heart.'

Drake's top lip curled. 'Three?'

She took a breath and let it out in a steady stream. 'He has to be open and not ashamed of showing his feelings.'

He gave a low grunt that could have been agreement or scorn or maybe a bit of both. 'Some men show their feelings too much. They have little or no emotional regulation. And their partners pay the price for it.'

'I guess you see a lot of that in your line of work. People behaving badly.'

'There's a saying amongst lawyers—we see bad people behaving badly and good people behaving badly.' He shifted the gears going around a corner and continued, 'What's number four?'

'He needs to be close to his family.'

Another gear change, this time a little more forceful. 'In proximity or emotionally?'

'Emotionally, of course.'

'Number five?'

'He has to want to have kids.'

Drake whistled through his teeth. 'You're right, I don't tick any boxes on your list.'

'You don't want kids? Ever?'

'No.'

'Because?'

He flicked her a brief glance. 'Kids get hurt when parents break up.'

'Not all parents break up.'

'Close to half do.'

'Yours didn't. They were still together when they had the accident, weren't they?'

Drake's jaw hardened and his grip on the gear stick tightened. 'What's your number six?'

Aerin was not so easily put off by his attempt to steer the conversation away from his background. It intrigued her why he was so reluctant to talk about it—or did that have something to do with having lost his family so young? But wouldn't he want to keep their memory alive by talking about them?

She realised she knew very little about his background other than the occasional snippets of information she had gleaned from her brother. But even Tom hadn't been all that forthcoming, and she hadn't wanted to appear *too* interested. All she knew was that his parents and younger sister had died in an accident when he was fifteen and he had been raised by relatives. It kind of explained his aura of self-sufficiency and hard-wired cynicism. He had loved and lost and had since learned not to rely on anyone but himself. 'Weren't your parents happy?'

There was a long drawn-out pause before

he spoke. 'No.' His tone had a flat, almost deadened note to it.

'Does it upset you to talk about your family?'

He let out a stiff curse word. 'What do you think?'

Aerin gave a soft sigh. 'I think it must be very hard to lose your entire family when you were so young. But how else will you remember them if you don't talk about them? Or is it just too painful?'

'It's...' his jaw worked for a moment and then he continued '...complicated and painful and I'd rather not talk about it.' He rearranged his shadowed features into a more relaxed pose as if he'd flicked a switch in his brain. End of subject. 'So, what's number six on your list?'

'My future partner has a dog or cat, or at least would like to have one.'

'Another tick against me.' Amusement coloured his tone but it wasn't reflected in his expression.

'But you like animals, right? You bent down to scratch Mr McPhee's dog, Mutley.'

Drake gave a dismissive shrug. 'I like animals and I like kids, but it doesn't mean I want them. What are we up to now? Number seven?'

'I want my partner to be musical or creative in some way.'

'I can play chopsticks and I draw a mean stick figure.'

Aerin fought back a smile. 'Be serious. Can you write poetry?'

'Not my forte, I'm afraid. So, what's number eight?'

'He has to love Christmas.'

There was another beat or two of silence.

'Let me guess,' Aerin said, looking at him again. 'You don't like the festive season. 'You've never once accepted my parents' and Tom's invitation to join us for Christmas.'

Drake had now parked the car and turned off the engine before he answered. 'Christmas isn't a time of joy for me.'

'Is that when you lost your family? At Christmas?'

'Christmas Eve.'

'Oh, Drake, I'm so sorry. That must have been so awful for you. I mean, to lose them at any time of year would be devastating but just before Christmas…it's such a family time.' How on earth had he coped with such a loss? Her heart ached at the thought of him all those years ago, suffering such sadness and trauma when he was only a teenager. No wonder he was so reluctant to talk about his family. It would be reopening a wound that hadn't quite healed…maybe it never would.

Drake glanced at the clock on the dashboard and then unclipped his seat belt. 'We need to get a move on. We can't have you missing your reunion, can we?'

Drake hadn't spoken to anyone of his family in years, not even his aunt who had looked after him until he was eighteen. Talking about them reminded him of his failure to protect his mother and sister. He carried the burden of guilt like a heavy yoke around his neck. A yoke that scratched and itched and rubbed his conscience raw. In hindsight, there had been clues about his father's criminal intentions, clues Drake had ignored because he had been lulled into a false sense of peace. His father was good at that—getting everyone, including Drake, to believe the storm was over and would not be returning. That *this* time, everything would change.

That his father would change. But his father had not changed, he had planned and plotted a devastating assault on the people he claimed to love most in the world. An assault Drake had missed by mere chance. A twist of fate that left him the last one standing with a burden of survivor guilt that was impossible to shake off.

There was a time when Christmas had been his favourite time of year. Not just for the anticipation of presents but he liked the tradition itself. The gathering of family, the celebration of being together, the nice food his mother so lovingly prepared. Now, he couldn't stand the sights and sounds and smell of Christmas. He wished he never had to see another Christmas tree with presents nestled around it for it reminded him of his family's tree with presents that had never been opened.

But somehow, Aerin with her gentle voice had coaxed out of him information he had shared with no one, not even her brother, Tom. He would have to remain vigilant around her this weekend for she had a way of getting under his guard. The proof of that was in the very fact she had got him to agree to the charade in the first place. He should not have agreed but if he hadn't taken her, someone who was less trustworthy might have and then he would have even more guilt to lug around.

A few minutes later, they had cleared security and then Drake led Aerin to a private boarding gate. 'I took the liberty of booking a private flight.'

Aerin stopped dead in her tracks to look up at him. 'But why? I mean, that would have cost a fortune and I don't mind travelling on a commercial flight.'

'If I was the type of guy to fall madly in love with someone, I'd want to spoil them, especially since I can afford it.'

Aerin cocked her head at him. 'Are you *sure* you're not a romantic at heart?'

Drake gave a deep rumble of laughter. 'Not a chance, Goldilocks. Now come on, your winged carriage awaits.'

CHAPTER THREE

AERIN TRIED NOT to look too impressed with the luxury of the private jet but since it was her first time in one, it was hard not to be a little wide-eyed and open-mouthed. The jet was decked out with two large cream-coloured leather seats in the front section with thick ankle-swallowing soft carpet on the floor. The next section had larger sofas running along each side of the jet with a large central coffee table, no doubt for conducting meetings or conferences in mid-air. There was a king-sized bedroom at the back end with its own bathroom, two other bathrooms situated at the front and rear of the aircraft.

There was a single flight attendant, a smartly dressed young man who issued them with drinks once they had taken their seats.

'Champagne for you, Ms Drysdale,'

Henry said. 'And iced water with a slice of lemon for Mr Cawthorn.'

'Oh, lovely, thank you,' Aerin said, taking the tall slim flute of fizzing bubbles off the silver tray.

Drake took his glass of water with a tight smile and the young man melted away and disappeared behind a sliding door that cordoned off the galley from the cabin.

Aerin swivelled in her seat to glance at him. 'You're not a fan of champagne?'

He put his glass of water on the table in front of their seats. 'I'm not a fan of alcohol, full stop.' He flashed her a wry smile and leaned back in his seat. 'Is that another point against me on your Mr Perfect checklist?'

'Not at all, it's just I didn't know that about you, that you don't drink, I mean.' She was surprised she hadn't noticed until now since he had been to her family's home on various social occasions. But given she mostly had tried to avoid him, it was no wonder she hadn't noticed whether he consumed alcohol or not.

'There's a lot you don't know about me.' His tone was mild and yet a fleeting shadow in his expression sent a tremor of disquiet through her.

'If we're going to be convincing this weekend, you'd better start filling me in a bit,' Aerin said. 'Why don't you drink?'

'It's a choice I made a long time ago.'

'Because of your family's accident? Was it a drunk driver or—?'

'No, they weren't killed by a drunk driver.' His jaw clenched for a moment and his eyes became hard, as if some memory from his past was stirring up emotions he didn't want to revisit. 'I drank when I was a lot younger but I never liked the taste. I only did it to be cool, to fit in, so I eventually made the decision to be a teetotaller.'

'My business partner Harper is a teetotaller too,' Aerin said. 'She had an alcoholic mother, so didn't want to risk it in case there was any genetic tendency for alcoholism. It was just as well since she had a cryptic pregnancy with Marli.' She waited a beat before adding, 'Were you close to your family?'

He picked up his glass of water and blotted some of the condensation away with the pad of his thumb. A brooding frown carved into his forehead and his mouth was set in a grim line. 'My mother and sister, yes, my father less so as time went on.'

'Why was that?'

He put the glass back down on the table in front of him and leaned back in his seat, his frown still in place. 'He wasn't the sort of man you could get close to.'

'Like you, you mean?'

Drake went completely still as if he had been snap-frozen. His expression was guarded, the drawbridge up on his emotions, but she could sense she had hit on a raw nerve with her comment.

'I'm sorry,' Aerin said into the silence. 'I didn't mean to upset you or anything…'

'You didn't upset me.' His relaxed tone didn't match the tension she could sense still lurking in his body.

'I'm guessing you don't like being compared to your father.'

'You're guessing right.'

Aerin wondered what made Drake so uncomfortable about being compared to his father. Not all sons had good relationships with their dads, even Tom had hit a rough patch in his teens with their dad. Their power struggle had gone on for a year or two until it eventually resolved as Tom had matured a bit more and their dad had loosened up.

But had Drake's father's untimely death meant he had never been able to enjoy getting closer to him? She could only imagine the guilt he would feel at never being able to fix things with his father. Many psychologists spoke of the father wound in modern men. Was Drake one of those men who carried deep emotional wounds from a distant, uninvolved father?

Aerin was wary of asking too many more deeply personal questions. She wanted their weekend together to work well in order to achieve her goal of satisfying her school friends that she had finally found a partner. But she also wanted the weekend to be positive for Drake, not an ordeal he had to endure.

On the other hand, there were things she needed to know about him in order for their charade to succeed this weekend. And there was a part of her that *wanted* to know more. She found him increasingly intriguing, like a complicated puzzle she was keen to solve. Her work required her to pay attention to every detail, from the tiniest to the largest and everything in between. Her powers of observation stood her in good stead for event planning but also gave her a talent for seeing and sensing things other people did not. And she was seeing and sensing things about Drake Cawthorn that demanded further investigation.

'I'm sorry for asking you so many questions but I need to know a little bit about you otherwise it will look strange to my friends. I'm a details person—I've always been like that. They would expect me to know everything there is to know about you.'

One side of his mouth came up in a cynical slant. 'Is that even possible? To know everything about a person? You can't. You can only know what they're willing to tell you. After that it's all guesswork.'

'Who did you go to live with after the accident? Your grandparents?'

'No, both my parents were estranged from their parents. I went to live with my aunt, my mother's older sister.'

'It must have been such a terrible time for you,' Aerin said. 'Were you badly injured in the accident?'

'I wasn't injured at all because I wasn't there.' There was a strange quality to his tone, a flat emptiness that seemed to echo with self-recrimination.

Her gaze went to the jagged scar on his left eyebrow. 'Oh? I thought that's where you must've got that scar and your crooked nose.'

Drake stroked one of his fingers across his scarred eyebrow. 'No, I got both of those in a fight when I was a teenager.' His expression still had a grim set to it as if he wasn't proud of that time in his life.

'You weren't in the car? I didn't realise that.' Aerin could only imagine the survivor guilt he must have felt, or still be feeling. If he had been in the car, he might not be alive today. The thought of him not existing made something deep in her chest ache. He had been a part of her life for so long she could not imagine life without him.

'No, I wasn't with them that day.' His voice still had that strange quality to it, an echo of regret, deep sadness and something else she couldn't put her finger on. She noticed his hands were clenched into fists against his strongly muscled thighs as if he was working hard to contain the emotions their conversation had stirred.

The pilot spoke at that moment through the intercom to inform them about the flight conditions and time of arrival. Aerin listened with one ear but she was still mulling over the things Drake had told her. She had always thought he had been in the car with his family—that was certainly the impression her brother had given her. She could only imagine the shock Drake would have experienced when informed of his parents' and sister's deaths. And how the sudden changes brought about by such a tragedy could impact a boy of fifteen.

The pilot stopped speaking and the jet began to taxi down the runway.

Aerin placed one of her hands over Drake's tightly fisted one resting on his thigh. 'I'm sorry if I stirred up sad memories for you by asking you so many questions.'

Drake looked at her hand on top of his for a beat or two. Then he placed his other hand over the top of hers and gently closed his fingers around hers. He turned his head and gave a crooked smile but there were shadows in his eyes that plucked at her heartstrings.

'It's okay, it was a long time ago and I've moved on.' His voice had a gravelly edge that hinted at the depth of emotion he was keeping contained.

Aerin's gaze drifted to his mouth and something flipped over in her stomach. His top lip was sensually contoured and his philtrum ridge between his nose and top lip was so well defined it could have been carved by a master sculptor. His lower lip was fuller than the top one and there was a shallow cleft in his chin partially hidden by his generously sprinkled dark stubble. She had a sudden urge to touch his regrowth with her fingers to experience its roughness against her softer skin. His broad-spanned hand was still anchoring her smaller one and the warmth of him seeped through her flesh like radiation. The heat travelled through her body, igniting a smouldering fire in her core.

His gaze drifted to her mouth, lingered there for a heart-stopping moment before returning to her gaze. His eyes moved between each of hers as if searching for something. Aerin suddenly realised she had never been this close to a man before. Close enough to see the individual pinpricks of stubble on his lean jaw. Close enough to see the flare of his ink-black pupils in the deep dark pools of his irises. Close enough to feel the soft waft of his warm breath against her face.

Aerin gave an audible swallow and sent the tip of her tongue across her lips. He followed the movement with his gaze, then one of his hands came up to the side of her face, cupping her cheek with a touch so gentle she shivered in reaction. His hooded gaze was focussed on her mouth, the ever so slight uptick in his breathing rate sending hers up as well.

'Are you going to…to kiss me?' Her voice came out breathless and a little rusty. *Please, please kiss me.* But of course she was too shy to say it out loud. She was too shocked that she actually *wanted* him to kiss her. It was a driving force building in her body, a wave of need she had never experienced before. A magnetic pull towards his mouth as if he had some sort of sensual power over her, drawing her inexorably closer. She had never wanted anyone to kiss her before now. And while Drake wasn't anywhere near her Mr Perfect, right then, all she could think about was feeling his firm lips against hers.

One side of his mouth tilted wryly. 'That would be flirting with danger, don't you think?'

She blinked and snatched in a much-needed breath. 'W-why is that?'

His hand cradling her cheek shifted to her chin, lifting it so her gaze was fixed on his. 'Because that wasn't part of the deal.'

The deal was a hands-off one but she suddenly realised how much she wanted him to kiss her. It was an urge, a desire she had never felt like this before. His mouth was a magnet drawing her like an iron filing. She wanted to feel those firm lips against hers, she wanted to experience her very first kiss from him. 'The deal?'

'We're not being observed right now.'

All the more reason she wanted him to kiss her. She didn't want her very first kiss to be watched by other people. She wanted it to be private and special and how could it be more special than with Drake? Someone she knew and trusted would not do the wrong thing by her. 'But I need to practise for when we are being observed.' She moistened her lips again and added, 'I've never actually been kissed before so what if I get it wrong?'

He released a puff of air through his wide nostrils, a heavy frown pulling at his forehead. 'Seriously? You've never been kissed?' The shock in his tone made her feel even more of a pariah than she already did.

Aerin pulled her hand out of his, and, checking the seat-belt light was off first, unclipped her seat belt and rose from the seat to put some distance between them. 'Go on, laugh at me. Mock me for being such a…a misfit.'

He unclipped his own belt and came over to her and took her hand again and stroked his thumb along the back of it. 'Hey, look at me.'

She met his concerned gaze and bit her lower lip. 'I know to someone like you who changes partners every week or two, I must seem like I've been dropped in from another century.'

Drake glanced at her mouth again and his other thumb began a slow stroke of her chin. His touch was gentle and yet electrifying, sending tingling sensations through her body. 'I'm a little gobsmacked you haven't been kissed before now, because I'm sure every man you've ever met has wanted to.'

'Including you?'

His mouth slanted in a smile. 'Are you flirting with me, Goldilocks?'

'I think I might be.' Aerin couldn't stop staring at his mouth. The sensual contours of it fascinated her. It was easily the most beautiful male mouth she had ever seen. She had seen his mouth so many times in the past, but it had never held the fascination it held for her now...or maybe it had but she had pretended not to notice. But now it was as if a switch had been turned on inside her brain and she couldn't turn it off.

She *wanted* to be kissed by him.

Desire had flicked into life inside her body as if a match had been struck against the dry tinder of her unmet needs. There was a flame building, spreading, heat lashing out in hungry tongues of fire, burning, burning, burning, wanting, wanting, wanting. Sending incendiary heat to every part of her body.

Drake lifted his hand to her hair and threaded his fingers through it, sending shivers skittering across her scalp and down her spine. His eyes were so dark she couldn't make out his pupils, his warm breath mingling intimately with hers. She got the sense he was at war with himself. One part of him tempted to kiss her, the other part holding back. And wasn't that true of her too? She had waited for so many years to experience the perfect kiss. Would it be a mistake to kiss Drake knowing he was nowhere near her Mr Perfect? But how could she resist him? He was the first man she had ever wanted to kiss.

He lowered his hand from her hair and captured one of hers. Aerin was conscious of every point of contact of his hand against hers, the slow stroke of his thumb on the back of her hand, his long fingers cupped around hers. She could smell the citrus notes of his aftershave with the understory of bergamot and wood, an intoxicating fragrance that stirred her senses into overdrive. Her gaze drifted to his mouth and her breath caught in her throat. Her eyes came back to his and something in the atmosphere changed. A tensing of the air, a crackling of electricity like the sudden surge of a high-voltage current.

Drake's eyes locked on hers. 'Once I kiss you, I can't un-kiss you. It will change our relationship, charade or no charade.'

Aerin swallowed again, heady anticipation building in every cell of her body. 'How will it change our relationship? It's just a kiss between…friends, isn't it?'

'Friends pretending to be lovers.'

Was he a friend? It wasn't easy to describe their relationship. She had never thought of him as a friend even though he had been in her life for so many years. Friends were people you loved and spent time with if and when you could, they were people you had things in common with and you were there for them and vice versa. Drake Cawthorn didn't quite fit that description and yet…and yet, he had come to her rescue this weekend.

'I've never really thought of you as a friend,' Aerin confessed. 'You're my brother's friend who I refer clients to for legal representation.'

His look was sardonic. 'Then why did you ask me to step in this weekend?'

She rolled her lips together. Why had she? 'I'm not sure… When Harper first suggested asking you, I was totally against the idea. In fact, I was horrified. But then I found myself near your office building the other day and I started to think about it a bit more. It made more and more sense to ask you rather than to ask a stranger. And...' she gave him a sheepish glance '... I was running out of time.'

Drake took one of her hands and brought it to within a couple of millimetres of his lips. 'Desperation makes all of us do things we later regret.' He moved his lips in a barely touching caress against her fingertips, sending a host of shivers cascading down her spine.

Aerin could feel her heart pounding as if it were going to crash through her chest wall. She was standing so close to him she could feel his body heat. She could feel the magnetic pull of him drawing her closer and closer and closer. She was mesmerised by his unwavering gaze, that bottomless brown gaze than saw so much but revealed so little. He lowered her hand from his lips and tugged her ever so gently towards him. She came in contact with the hard wall of his chest and the cradle of his hips, and a shock wave of lust rocked through her.

His mouth came down, down, down until it was almost touching hers. 'Are you sure about this?' he asked in a deep rough-around-the-edges voice.

'I'm sure.' And she was, totally sure that it was his mouth she wanted to be the first to kiss her. It didn't make sense in some ways and yet in others it did. He wasn't soulmate material, he didn't tick any of the boxes on her checklist but, at that moment, all she wanted was the firm press of his lips on hers. She wanted it like a forbidden drug— a drug that might not be good for her in the long run but, oh, how much did she crave it right now.

Drake's mouth came down and pressed against hers in a light-as-air kiss. It was a soft, momentary touchdown and yet it sent a tremor of greedy want through her body. He pressed his lips back down on hers, moving them against her mouth in a gentle massaging movement that set her pulse racing. She murmured her approval against his lips, instinctively leaning into him in an effort to get closer.

His arms came around her, drawing her against his body, one hand at the small of her back, the other cradling the side of her face. He stroked his tongue along the seam of her mouth and she opened to him, welcoming him in with another breathless sigh of pleasure. He tasted clean and fresh and exotic at the same time, his tongue commanding as it called hers into sensual play. She touched her tongue against his and a lightning-fast bolt of heat went straight to her core. He deepened the kiss, angling his head to gain better access, his hand on the small of her back pressing her even closer to the hardened ridge of his stirring male flesh. A thrill went through her to think she had turned him on, that it wasn't just her attracted to him but a mutual thing that flared between them.

Aerin slid her hands up his chest and then around his neck, her fingers playing with his hair where it brushed his collar. He made a guttural sound and kissed her harder, more urgently, his tongue duelling with hers in an erotic battle that stirred her senses into a madcap frenzy. His breathing rate escalated along with hers, the explosive heat of his kiss making her dizzy with need.

Drake finally lifted his mouth off hers

and looked down at her with a slightly dazed look in his eyes. But then he rapid-blinked and adopted his customary sardonic smile. 'How did I measure up?'

She looked at him blankly. 'Measure up?'

'You've waited a long time to be kissed. Did my performance meet your high expectations?'

Aerin was a little stung by his choice of words. Here she was thinking he was as swept away by their kiss as she was and yet it had been nothing more than a performance on his part? She stepped away from him and went back to her seat, clipping her seat belt on with a definitive snap. 'It was... okay, I guess.'

There was a beat or two of silence.

Drake resumed his seat beside her and took one of her hands in his. 'Hey, that was a little insensitive of me. I'm sorry.' He stroked his fingers across the back of her hand in a touch so light it was almost ticklish. 'The thing is...' he hesitated for another beat, his gaze meeting hers '... I was enjoying it a little too much.'

'You were?'

His expression was rueful. 'You couldn't tell?'

Aerin could feel warmth spreading over her cheeks and another even warmer sensation flowing to her core. 'I'm glad the kiss wasn't a one-way affair.'

His mouth tilted in a smile. 'It certainly wasn't.'

Aerin lifted her hand and traced over the jagged scar on his left eyebrow, then she stroked the same finger down the crooked slope of his nose. 'Did it hurt?' Her voice came out soft and a little breathless, for touching him sent a wave of longing through her that shocked her in its intensity.

'Like hell.'

She stroked his nose again. 'You didn't consider having surgery to straighten it?'

'No.'

'How did the other guy fare?'

Drake's mouth twisted and he took her hand again, his thumb resuming its gentle stroking on the back of her hand. 'I was seriously outclassed. He was bigger, meaner, stronger and fought dirty. I didn't stand a chance.'

Aerin frowned at the thought of such an

ugly fight. 'You were lucky you weren't killed.'

Something flashed in his gaze and his mouth twisted even further. 'Yes, I was. Very lucky.'

CHAPTER FOUR

DRAKE WAS GLAD the flight was a short one because sitting so close to Aerin after kissing her had stirred his senses into overdrive. Hot flickers of lust still tingled through his body and all he could think of was kissing her again. He relived every moment of her lips beneath his, the softness of her, the sweetness, the exotic taste that set fire to his blood.

You're the first man to kiss her...

He tried not to think too deeply about that but how could he not? Aerin had waited until now to be kissed—by him. Why? Because he was familiar to her and not a total stranger? Because she felt the current of sensual energy that had first pulsed between them in his office the other day? But getting too close and personal was not good for either of them. This weekend was a charade, not a fling in the real sense. He could not allow himself to get close to her or anyone. But somehow she had teased out of him more about himself than he had told anyone—even the counsellor he was forced to see when he was a teenager.

Drake was all too aware of the danger of catching feelings, which was why he only ever dated women for short periods. And while a weekend hanging out with Aerin was hardly a long time, it was still full of emotional potholes. He already had a relationship of sorts with her, which had been strictly platonic until the moment his mouth touched hers.

Something had changed in that moment. A change he'd felt ripple through his entire body as if it were being reprogrammed. It might have been Aerin's first kiss but in a strange way it had felt like that for him too. The soft shy press of her lips against his had sent fireworks through his blood. The sweet and yet exciting taste of her igniting a ferocious desire in him like an addict reacting to a forbidden drug. One taste had made him greedy for more.

But he was *not* going to have more.

Drake was a man who knew how to control himself. He had worked long and hard at regulating his emotions, having seen first-hand how dangerous it was when others chose not to. He bore the physical scars of showdowns with his father as a young teenager. His feeble attempts to protect his mother and sister had done nothing in the end, only left him with scars and deep emotional wounds and a nagging sense of failure. He had failed to protect his mother and sister. He had loved and yet lost them.

He would *not* love again.

'You're finally here!' Bella, one of Aerin's school friends, greeted them in the foyer of the stately home they had hired for the weekend. 'And you must be Drake. I can't tell you how excited we all are to finally meet you.'

Aerin was conscious of the warm band of Drake's arm around her waist. And conscious of the speculative and excited gazes of her friends. Bella, Julia, Suzy and Chantal were each arm in arm with their own partners and it only reinforced her conviction that using Drake as a stand-in date was the right thing to do. She could not have borne the weekend sans partner. Her friends were all so happy in their relationships and as this was their last reunion before Julia moved to Australia, it was even more important everything was perfect. But…there was a big part of her that felt uneasy about the game she was playing. The kiss between her and Drake on the private jet he had arranged had stirred sensations in her that troubled her. Not because the kiss wasn't perfect—it was, in every way. But he wasn't after the things she was after and this thing between them was only a charade.

Aerin painted a blissfully happy smile on her face—not all that hard to do after that kiss. Her lips had only just stopped tingling, but the rest of her body had not. It was quietly thrumming away as if a potent drug had been injected into her veins. Drake's slightest touch sent her senses spinning and standing so close to him made her ache to get even closer.

'Thank you,' Drake said in his deep baritone. 'It's great to meet you all too.'

After all the hugs and air kisses and handshakes and introductions were out of the way, Aerin went with Drake to their room in order to get ready for dinner.

'Here we go,' Drake said, opening the door to their suite, which was quite a way from the other guests. 'The Blue Room.'

Aerin stepped over the threshold and turned in a circle to take in the décor and priceless-looking antiques, including a four-poster bed. 'It's like stepping back in time, isn't it?'

A frown was pulling at Drake's forehead. 'Did you happen to notice a sofa anywhere?'

Aerin glanced around the room but apart from a couple of spindly chairs, a writing desk and a loveseat there was no sofa. 'Maybe there's another room through here...' She opened the door but it proved to be the en suite. 'Oh, that's the bathroom.'

'We have a problem.'

'We do? I mean, of course we do.' Aerin's cheeks flared with heat hot enough to warm the room.

His eyes meshed with hers for a heart-stopping moment. 'I'll sleep on the floor.'

'That won't be very comfortable for you. I don't mind if you share the bed, I mean, not in that way, I meant you on one side, me on the other.'

One side of his mouth lifted in a half-smile that did serious damage to her already skyrocketing pulse rate. 'Can I trust you to keep your hands to yourself?'

Aerin gave him a mock gimlet glare. 'I didn't force myself on you. You kissed me quite willingly, if I recall.'

His eyes darkened. 'I did indeed.'

Aerin let out a wobbly breath and shifted her gaze from his and went to open her overnight bag. 'We have half an hour before dinner.'

'I'll go for a quick walk to give you some privacy.'

Aerin pulled out her navy-blue velvet evening dress and shook out the creases, glancing at him again. 'But won't the others think that's a bit strange? It's dark outside anyway. Besides, I can get changed in the bathroom.'

'Aerin.' The sombre note was back in his voice. 'You're safe with me, no matter what.'

'I know that. It's why I asked you to be here this weekend instead of someone I don't know and trust.'

His smile was wry. 'You trust me even after that kiss?'

Her gaze drifted to his mouth and her heart jumped in her chest like a startled frog. 'Yes, I trust you.' She licked her suddenly dry lips and hugged her dress close to her chest. 'I'm not so sure I trust myself, though.'

His kiss had made her hungry for more. How was she going to resist him? Why *should* she resist him? The sensuality he awakened in her was empowering. It made her realise how much she had been missing out on in being so cautious about dating. This was her chance to experiment a little. He wasn't Mr Perfect, but it didn't mean she couldn't enjoy a short dalliance with him. Or was she rationalising too much? Talking herself into a fling with him because she knew he would give her nothing but a fling?

Drake was standing within touching distance of her but she had no idea which of them had moved or if both of them had. He sent one of his hands down the length of her arm in a lazy caress and even through the layers of her clothes her body leapt and tingled at his touch. 'The kissing and touch-

ing can't go any further than this weekend.'
His fingers had got to the bare skin of her
hand in a light as air touch that sent a shiver
down her spine.

'I know.'

His eyes searched hers for a pulsing moment. 'I'm not what you're looking for.'

'I know.' Did he have to keep remind-
ing her? He didn't tick any of her boxes and
yet…and yet…that kiss. *Gulp.* She couldn't
get it out of her mind. Couldn't wait to feel
his lips on hers again.

His gaze lowered to her mouth and lingered there for a beat or two. Then he drew
in a deep breath and released it in a jagged
stream and finally brought his eyes back
to hers. Dark, intense, determined and yet
a shadow of something else lurking there.
'How long will it take you to get ready?'

'Five, ten minutes?'

'Take your time. I'll catch up on a couple
of emails. Pretend I'm not here.'

*Yeah, right, like that was going to be easy
to do.*

Aerin draped her dress over one arm and,
snatching up her make-up kit with her other
hand, disappeared into the bathroom.

Drake pinged back a couple of short emails, but his mind was well and truly in the bathroom with Aerin. He pictured her changing out of her travel clothes and into that stunning blue velvet dress she'd brought with her. She would look elegant dressed in a bin liner, but that midnight shade of blue was a perfect foil for her grey-blue eyes and creamy complexion.

He tossed his phone to one side and quickly changed into the tux he'd brought with him. He was about to tie his bow tie when Aerin came out of the bathroom. His hands fell away from his neck and his breath stalled in his chest. She had bundled her long hair into a makeshift bun at the back of her head that highlighted the elegant length of her neck. Some dangling sapphire and diamond earrings glittered from her delicate earlobes. Her make-up was subtle and yet made the most of her features—the smoky eye make-up, the shiny lip-gloss, the blush and highlighter on her aristocratic cheekbones turning her into a princess fit for a ball.

Her dress was even more stunning on her than he had imagined. The off-the-shoulder style clung to her slim frame in all the right places—places he wanted to touch and caress. Places he had forbidden himself to touch and caress. Places he knew would take every ounce of willpower and then some *not* to touch and caress. *Sheesh.* Why did he agree to this? It was madness to think kissing her wouldn't change anything. Of course it changed everything. He could not get her mouth out of his mind, her taste off his tongue and his desire, meanwhile, was still thrumming like a background beat in his blood.

'You look…amazing…' As a high-powered lawyer, it was rare for him to be lost for words but right then Drake could barely get a full sentence out.

Aerin gave a tentative smile, her cheeks going a delightful shade of pink. She swished from side to side and the skirt of the dress swirled like a blue wave around her. 'Do you think so? I wasn't sure about the off-the-shoulder style. I normally don't show this much flesh.'

'You look stunning.' He was having trouble keeping his eyes away from her small but perfect cleavage.

'Could you help me put this on?' She opened her palm to reveal a fine gold chain with a sapphire and diamond pendant on it. 'The fastening is too fiddly for me to put on by myself.'

Drake took the pendant from her hand. 'Turn around.' He came up close behind her and looped the chain around her neck. Her flowery perfume teased his nostrils and dazzled his senses, the fragrance redolent of a summer garden. He wanted to bury his head beside her neck and breathe more of her in. He frowned in concentration as he worked to fasten the catch, but the chain and its clasp were tiny and it didn't help that his hands weren't as steady as he would have liked. And nor was his heart rate. Damn it.

'It's a tricky fastening,' Aerin said in a husky tone.

'I think I need to get my eyes checked. There, that's it.' He stepped back and she turned around to face him. The pendant glinted from just above her cleavage.

'Thanks.' Her hand went to the pendant and shifted it back and forth along its chain. 'My grandmother gave it to me for my last birthday, along with the earrings.'

'They're very beautiful. And so are you.'

Her blush deepened and her hand fell away from the pendant. 'Thank you.' She glanced at his as yet untied bow tie. 'Do you need some help with that?'

Drake didn't but he couldn't resist the opportunity for her to touch him, even if it was simply to do up his bow tie. 'Go for it. I'm too much of a snob to buy one of those clip-on ones.'

Aerin stepped closer and he breathed in another heady draught of her fragrance. He would never be able to look at a rose or a sweet pea again without thinking of her. She took the ends of his bow tie and deftly knotted it around his neck. The movement of her fingers so close to his neck sent shivers rolling down his spine. He could not stop thinking of those soft little hands moving on other parts of his body. A low rumble of lust moved through his blood like a distant earthquake, sending shock waves and tremors through his entire body. How was he supposed to keep his hands off her when all he wanted was to draw her close and kiss that delectable mouth? To crush her slim frame to his hard one and feel every feminine curve stir his body into fervent heat?

Once she had completed tying the bow tie, she patted his chest with one of her hands. 'There you go.'

Drake caught her hand before she could step back, holding it against the *tump-tump-tump* of his heart. His eyes held hers in a silent lock, her pupils instantly flaring like pools of ink. The point of her tongue slipped out to sweep over her lips, and a rocket blast of lust slammed him in the groin.

Drake drew in a shuddering breath. 'I told myself I wasn't going to do this again.'

Her look was innocent and yet her words were breathlessly delivered. 'Do what?'

He gave a rueful smile. 'You know what.'

'You want to kiss me again?'

He brushed an imaginary hair away from her forehead. 'Don't sound so surprised, Goldilocks. I can't get our first kiss out of my mind.'

'It was my first kiss, not yours. You've probably kissed hundreds of women.'

'No one like you.' Drake lifted her hand to his mouth and kissed the backs of her bent knuckles, his eyes holding hers.

She shivered and moved a little closer as if unable to withstand the magnetic pull of attraction, the same magnetic pull he was feeling towards her. 'Why no one like me? Am I so different from everyone you normally date?'

'Different in too many ways to list.' Drake let go of her hand and gave a crooked smile. 'Now, we'd better get to the dinner before they think we've been waylaid up here doing something else.'

A vivid blush swept across her cheeks and she turned away to check her reflection in the mirror, catching his gaze for a brief moment before repositioning the pendant around her neck.

'I feel bad about lying to my friends. I know I should've just been honest and told them I haven't found the love of my life yet but I don't want our last reunion to be all about me and my high expectations and so far unfulfilled dreams.' She let out a long sigh and added, 'I wish I didn't have to stay the whole weekend. I'm not good at acting, or lying for that matter, which in our case amounts to the same thing. I'm worried I'm going to make a fool of myself in front of them all.'

Drake came over to her to stand behind her, meeting her eyes in the mirror once more. He placed his hands on her bare shoulders and tried to ignore the rush of heat burning in his groin. 'We don't have to stay the whole weekend. We can stay for the dinner and overnight and then leave first thing. We can tell them we're heading someplace else for a bit of couple time.' Even as he was saying the words, a red flag was waving in his head. But he found he wanted to be alone with her, not surrounded by her friends and their partners, but just to be with her.

Her grey-blue eyes widened. 'You'd be okay with that? I mean, heading somewhere else tomorrow?'

'Sure. It will take the pressure off us both, pretending all the time to be something we're not.' He should *not* be okay with it. He should be telling her no, no, no, we shouldn't be alone together. Not totally alone. But somehow he couldn't find the words to say it. The desire to do the opposite was taking command of the control centre of his brain. His brain that was normally so rational and logical and risk averse and here he was suggesting a secret getaway.

Just the two of them.

And if that wasn't a risk, he didn't know what the hell was.

But wasn't pretending to be lovers in the company of others worse? At least if they were alone the pressure would be off. They could just hang out as friends and enjoy each other's company without worrying about giving off the wrong vibe or something. Besides, the more he acted like a lover around her, the more he wanted to *be* her lover. He was wary of allowing the charade to go too far, to drift from an act into reality. He was aware of how slim the divide was between pretending to feel passion to actually feeling it. And he did feel it. He had not stopped feeling it from the moment she'd turned up outside his office that day. The trick for him was how to turn it off before someone got hurt.

Aerin turned to face him and he had to force his hands away from her shoulders, when all he wanted was to bring her closer. He opened and closed his fingers to try and stop them from tingling from touching her silken skin. But touching her had sent his blood on a low simmer and he knew it wouldn't take much for a flame to leap into life.

'Drake, you've been so good about this situation. It's a perfect solution now that I think of it. It will reduce the risk of one of the girls taking photos that end up on social media. We can explain we want some time alone before we make any announcement about our relationship to our friends and family.'

Drake was glad she couldn't read his mind at that point. He was still wondering how he was going to get through the night in this room with her. He prided himself on his self-control, but she was a temptation he had not been prepared for.

And he was *always* someone who was prepared.

But this time…not so much.

CHAPTER FIVE

AERIN ENJOYED THE dinner dance much more than she had in years gone past. It was lovely being part of a couple, even though she and Drake, strictly speaking, were not a couple. They were acting. But every now and then he would glance her way and smile and her heart would lift like a helium balloon in her chest. Everyone was in a joyous mood and the chatter around the table as dinner was served was lively and convivial. Drake occasionally contributed in his charming and relaxed way, but for the most part he quietly observed the others without revealing too much about himself.

Chantal leaned close at one point to talk to Aerin, while her partner Taddeo chatted to Drake about a business investment he had planned in the IT sector.

'Aerin, I'm so thrilled you and Drake

got together,' Chantal said. 'How long have you been seeing each other? What does your brother think? Tom must be feeling pretty chuffed about you two hitting it off at last. And your parents. You've always had such high standards when it came to men. I thought you didn't even like Drake. You used to turn your nose up whenever his name was mentioned in the past.'

Aerin decided it was best to stay as close to the truth as possible because Chantal, as a long-term school friend, knew a lot more about her than a casual acquaintance, even though they were not as close as Aerin was to Harper and Ruby. 'It's too early to say where our relationship is going but that's why we're keeping it quiet for now.'

'Well, I think he's gorgeous,' Chantal said. 'And the way he looks at you just about melts my heart.' She gave a dreamy sigh and added, 'God, I love seeing a man fall and fall hard.'

Mmm... Well, it did seem Drake was doing an award-winning performance of playing the besotted man in love. Aerin only hoped she was doing an equally stellar job. She cast her gaze in Drake's direction and smiled and he smiled back and gave a cheeky wink that sent a hot wave of colour through her cheeks, not to mention her lower body.

But how much on her part was acting?

Aerin was starting to see him in a new light. The more time she spent with him, the more she realised how she had misjudged him in the past. His cynicism hid a sensitivity he didn't want anyone to see. His determination not to fall in love hinted at a man who was shy of commitment because he wanted to avoid the pain of a break-up. It didn't mean he couldn't love but rather he chose not to.

Finally, the dinner was over and the dancing began. And instead of being a wallflower as she had been every year in the past, this time she was in Drake's arms being spun around the floor as if they were the star performers at a dance academy.

'I didn't know you could dance so well,' Aerin said, somewhat breathlessly as they did a fast-paced circuit of the floor, somehow, rather miraculously, she thought, avoiding colliding into all the other couples.

'Look who's talking.' Drake drew her

even closer to the hard frame of his body, his pelvis flush against hers. Hot tingles shot down her spine and her heart rate picked up, which had nothing to do with the energetic dancing. Being close to him stirred sensations in her she had never felt before. It was as if he lit a fire in her blood, a fire that smouldered and simmered and flickered with hot flames of lust. A lust she didn't know how to control. It had never been part of her plan to have a fling with someone. She wanted to fall in love with the love of her life. Flings were temporary and casual, and nothing about how she envisaged her life going forward was temporary or casual. She wanted for-ever love. Total commitment, till death do us part love. But being with Drake made her question the strict code she had lived by. Maybe it was time for her to loosen up a bit. To explore the chemistry that had fired between them.

Aerin laughed. 'You're way too generous in your praise. I stepped on your toes at least three times back there.'

He grinned down at her. 'I didn't notice.'

The air was suddenly charged with a current of electricity that seemed to pulse between their locked gazes. *Fizzzt. Fizzzt. Fizzzt.* A current Aerin could feel in her body from her head to her toe and to each of her fingertips.

Aerin was aware of the broad span of Drake's hand resting on the small of her back, the heat like a brand searing her flesh, warming her blood to boiling. A low deep throb drummed in her body, a call of nature so primitive and primal it was overwhelming.

Drake's eyes darkened to obsidian and he bent his head lower, so his mouth was within touching distance of hers. He hovered there for an infinitesimal moment, which only ratcheted up her need to feel his lips on hers.

'Kiss me…' Her words came out on a barely audible whisper that, given the loud music playing, he couldn't possibly have heard with any clarity. But then his mouth came down and set hers alight as if he sensed her need for him.

Drake's lips closed over hers in a light press of flesh on flesh that sent a rocket blast through her blood. One of his hands came up to cradle the side of her face, the other remained in the small of her back, holding her to the burgeoning heat of his hardening male body. A blooming spreading heat that ignited her feminine flesh like a match on tinder, flames of need racing out of control to every erogenous zone in her body.

Drake finally lifted his mouth off hers and gazed down at her with a lopsided smile and glittering eyes. His hand still cradling the side of her face, his thumb stroking her cheek in a gentle caress that made her spine turn to liquid. 'Would it upset everyone if we left tonight instead of in the morning? I know a place only an hour or so away but it's completely private and that way you can have your own room.'

Aerin knew she shouldn't be feeling such a deep pang of disappointment about him insisting on her having her own room. For close to thirty years she had never shared a room with anyone other than the occasional sleepover with a girlfriend or two. But at the heart of his suggestion was his concern for her comfort and that meant a lot to her. 'But what will we tell them? I mean, about why we're not staying here?'

'I'll tell them I've planned a romantic getaway for the two of us. A remote cottage near a loch and no neighbours for miles around.'

Aerin tilted her head on one side, studying him as if he were a complicated puzzle. 'It does indeed sound very romantic. But aren't you worried they might think you're taking me away to propose to me or something?'

Drake shrugged one broad shoulder. 'We both know that's not going to happen.'

Yes, well, she didn't want him to propose since he didn't tick any of her boxes but did he have to be so adamantly blunt about it? Aerin painted a smile on her face. 'Do you know CPR?'

'Yep, why?'

'Because if by some miracle you did get down on bended knee, I would have a heart attack on the spot.'

Drake smiled with his mouth but not with his eyes. 'If by some miracle you said yes, I would too.'

As it turned out, no one was all that surprised by Drake's plan to whisk Aerin away for the rest of the weekend. The girls and their partners farewelled them as if they were indeed leaving for their honeymoon, with whoops and cheers and waves.

Drake drove through the moonlit night, glancing at her from time to time. 'Why don't you lay your head back and have a sleep? It'll be an hour before we get there.'

Aerin tried but failed to disguise a yawn, quickly covering her mouth with her hand. 'Sorry. I am a bit knackered. I don't think I've danced that much in years, actually ever.'

'Acting, too, can make you pretty tired.'

Aerin chewed his statement over for a beat or two. Had he found it trying to pretend all evening he was in love with her in front of her school friends and their partners? Had he hated every minute of it? If so, he had hidden it well. 'Yes, it can. Was it awful for you to pretend to be in love with me for the evening? Chantal was convinced you were head over heels for me.'

It was too dark inside the car for her to see his features clearly, but she caught a glint of something in his eyes reflected off the moonlight. 'People see what they want to see, especially when they've had plenty of alcohol.'

'Yes, well, there was a lot of champagne consumed.' She disguised another yawn and added sleepily, 'I might just close my eyes for a bit. Wake me if you want me to take over the wheel at some point.'

'I'm not used to letting anyone drive me. Call me a control freak but that's just the way I live my life.'

Aerin was tired but not so tired she couldn't hear the note of determination in his voice. She turned her head where it was resting against the headrest to glance at him again. 'Because of the accident?'

There was a long silence. A silence that contained a strange energy, as if a ghost had suddenly joined them in the car. A shiver ran over Aerin's skin and she pulled her evening wrap closer around her shoulders.

'It wasn't an accident.' Drake's voice was heavy, weighed down with something she had not heard in it before.

Aerin sat up straighter in her seat, her earlier tiredness falling away leaving her open-eyed and fully alert. 'What do you mean?'

His mouth was twisted in a grimace. 'My mother and sister didn't die in a car crash.'

She swallowed tightly. 'How did they die?' Her voice came out in a shocked whisper.

Drake shifted the car's gears to take a sweeping bend that climbed further into the hills of the countryside. He drove competently and yet there was an underlying anger in his movements, an anger she could sense he fought hard to control. 'They were murdered.'

The words dropped into the car like a pulled grenade. Words Aerin had not expected. Words that were so shocking, so brutally shocking she couldn't process them in her brain. It was like being stunned by a physical blow to the head. Her brain was spinning without traction, none of her thoughts finding a foothold. Drake's family had been murdered? How had he lived with such dreadful pain? A car crash would have been tragic enough, but to have your entire family murdered by someone was just beyond bearing. How could anyone recover from such dreadful grief? Could you ever recover?

But then something did take hold in her brain as she recalled his statement: *'My mother and sister didn't die in a car crash.'*

What about his father? Nothing was making sense. Everything she had been told about his family over the years—the little she had been told—was not true.

'I'm sorry,' Drake said after a long moment, his voice rough and heavy with regret, perhaps, she thought, even a little self-loathing. 'I shouldn't have told you.'

Aerin swept her tongue over her parchment-dry lips, her hands not quite steady in her lap. 'What about your father? You said your mother and sister were…murdered…' Even saying the word was horrifying to her. Of course one read about murders in the news every day but when you actually met someone who had lost someone they loved in such a despicable way, it made one realise the tragic enormity of such a loss.

'Please,' Drake said. 'Forget I said anything. It's not something I want to talk about. Ever. With anyone.'

'Does Tom know?'

'No.'

Another beat or two of silence passed. Aerin imagined she could hear her own heartbeat thumping in her chest like a drum.

She could certainly feel the pulse of her blood hammering in her veins.

'Why not? I mean, why didn't you tell Tom? You've been friends for years.'

'Because I chose not to tell anyone about what happened that day.'

And yet he had told her. Not all of it but enough for her to ache to know more.

Aerin ran one of her hands through her hair, part of her up-do tumbling from its restraining clip. It was only as she put her hand back in her lap that she saw it was shaking. 'Oh, Drake, I don't know what to say. I want you to tell me everything, but I understand how awfully painful that must be for you. I can't get my head around what you've told me so far. I don't know how you've managed to cope with such a terrible situation. God, you were only fifteen…'

Drake changed gears to drive up a long, wooded driveway that led to a cottage on the top of a hill. The cottage was bathed in moonlight, the loch below it past the dark looming shadows of the woods picture-postcard perfect. A light breeze crinkled the surface of the water like a bolt of silver silk.

Drake's forehead was as crinkled as the

loch, his eyes focussed on the driveway, his hands clenched on the steering wheel. His jaw locked. He brought the car to a stop in front of the stone cottage that was larger than it first appeared. He turned off the engine and released a long breath and turned to look at her in the moonlit darkness.

'Thank you.'

'For what?'

'For not hounding me for more information,' Drake said.

Aerin moistened her lips again. If only he knew how much she wanted to. But she was not a pushy person by nature and understood people had to be ready to reveal things. They had to develop a level of trust. They had to feel ready to share such sadness with a safe person. A trustworthy and safe person. But it saddened her to think not her even her brother, Tom, knew the full story. What did that say about her brother? Or was it that Drake didn't allow himself to trust anyone? That he didn't feel safe with anyone? 'I guess if you really wanted to tell someone, anyone, you would have done it by now.'

Drake reached out his hand and picked up

one of her loosened strands of hair that had fallen from its up-do. 'You've let your hair down.' There was a wry quality to his tone and a twist to his mouth that made him all the more attractive. So attractive, she mentally ticked number one of her soulmate checklist: *tall, dark and handsome.*

Aerin couldn't keep her gaze from drifting to his mouth. She sucked in a shuddery breath and was suddenly conscious of the close confines of the car. She could smell the citrussy tang of his aftershave—a smell that was so tantalising to her senses she could feel herself melting. She could smell the warm minty freshness of his breath. Could feel the thrum of desire beating between her legs and wondered if he was feeling the same.

His eyes darkened to pitch and his head came down, his mouth covering hers in a brief kiss that was gossamer-soft. But as he lifted away, his lips clung to hers as a silky cobweb did to a dry surface. He gave a muttered groan that sounded like a curse and covered her mouth once more. Aerin breathlessly submitted to the commanding stroke of his tongue, her lips parting on a sigh, her heart thumping with delight, her arms snaking around his neck, her fingers playing with the thick strands of his closely cropped hair.

The kiss went on and on, sending shivers of reaction down her spine. Something about the darkness outside tinged with silvery moonlight gave it a magical quality, as if Aerin had stepped into a fairy tale. She was swept up in the moment, enjoying the roughness of his skin against her face, enjoying the more and more urgent sound of his breathing, the strengthening of his hold, as if he never wanted to let her go.

Drake's hands came up to cradle both sides of her face in a touch so gentle it made her heart squeeze. He angled his head to deepen the kiss, another deep, rough groan sounding in his throat. Aerin responded by meeting his tongue with hers, playfully dancing and duelling until her blood was simmering with need.

He pulled away to gaze down at her in the semi-darkness. 'I didn't bring you all the way up here to seduce you.' Another wry twist to his lips and he added, 'But kissing you is becoming a bit of an addiction, I'm afraid.'

Aerin traced her fingertip around the contour of his mouth with a feather-light touch. 'I guess there are worse addictions, right?' She tried to keep her tone playful but all she could think about was wanting his mouth back on hers.

'Yes.' Drake put her from him and opened the car door and a blast of chilly air entered the car.

But even so, Aerin still burned for him deep in her feminine core. His passionate kiss had stirred her senses to life and she realised she wanted more than his kisses. Much more. But how could she ask him to be her lover when he wasn't interested in settling down in the future? Wouldn't that be compromising on everything she had written on her checklist? Her plan for her life. She wasn't the type of person to have flings and that was all it could ever be between them because that was the only type of relationship he ever had. Wasn't it naïve of her to think he might change for her?

Within a few minutes, they were inside the quaint two-storey cottage. Drake carried in their bags and placed them in each of the two bedrooms, while Aerin set to making a warm drink in the kitchen. She heard the movement of Drake's firm tread upstairs and her mind wandered... The cottage was a lovely place to spend time with a lover. So cosy, so private, so intimate. He had seemed to organise the booking of it with incredible speed. Had he brought someone else here in the past? Or did he or a friend own it? Had he brought her here because he could not bear the thought of spending the night in the same room as her back at the reunion hotel?

Aerin heard him come back down the stairs and then enter the sitting room. She had noticed a fire had been laid in the hearth on her quick tour around when they'd first arrived. She carried two drinks on a tray and entered the sitting room, where Drake was kneeling on one knee in front of the fireplace, frowning at the now flickering flames.

He glanced over his shoulder as she came in, his frown relaxing on his forehead, but she could still see a shadow of it in his dark eyes. 'Thanks for making the drinks. I've put you in the room overlooking the forest. It's the only bedroom with a lock on the door. I'm further down the hall.'

Aerin set the tray down on the table situated a metre or so in front of the fireplace, near the twin sofas. 'You think I don't trust you?' If only he knew it was herself she didn't trust. He had awakened needs in her she hadn't known she possessed, or at least not to that intensity. His kisses had stirred her into blazing heat like the fire he had just lit in the fireplace.

Drake straightened from in front of the hearth and then took one of the mugs from the tray on the coffee table, his expression inscrutable. 'I've been around people most of my life who say one thing and do the complete opposite. I want you to feel one hundred per cent safe with me.'

She took her own mug and sat cross-legged on one of the sofas. 'I do, Drake.' Her voice came out softer and huskier than she'd planned. She toyed with the handle of her mug and then added, 'Have you brought a lover here in the past? You managed to book it at short notice, so I thought maybe you either owned it or were familiar with it from previous visits.'

One side of his mouth tilted wryly. 'I do own it but I haven't brought anyone here before. I've only had it a few months.' He put his mug on the mantelpiece and added, 'It's one of several secluded properties I've bought for a women's shelter charity I set up a few years ago.'

Aerin cradled her mug between her hands, unable to take her eyes off his face that was so enhanced by the flickering flames of the fire behind him. He looked like a hero out of a Jane Austen or Charlotte Brontë novel—inscrutable, darkly handsome and intriguing. 'So, it's used as a shelter for women and children who need to escape their violent partners? But it's so incredibly isolated. Wouldn't that be scary for a woman in fear of her life?'

'It's not as isolated as you might think. The local police are on speed dial on the security pad over there.' He pointed to the security system panel she had noticed in every room but not taken too much notice of before. 'They would be here within minutes if needed. But this cottage is more of a holiday retreat for families who need healing time after the threat has been taken care of.'

'You mean once the perpetrator is in custody?'

'Yes.'

There was a long silence with only the sound of the flames flickering in the fireplace and the wind whistling outside.

Drake had turned back to stare at the fire and it gave Aerin a chance to study him again. He was frowning but in a brooding sort of way, as if some memories were troubling him. Memories triggered by their conversations in the car earlier and now. But how could she press him for more details of his background without appearing insensitive? He had told her repeatedly he didn't want to discuss his past.

Aerin leaned forward to put her mug down on the coffee table. 'Drake... I think it's amazing how much you help people. I had no idea you'd set up such a wonderful charity. I have to admit, I found your choice of legal speciality in prenuptial agreements a bit off-putting, a little cynical on your part. But I guess you've seen first-hand how difficult it is for women who have been financially disadvantaged in a divorce or break-up.'

Drake moved away from the fire as if the heat was getting too much for him. Even she could feel the warmth from her position on the sofa—waves of warmth that gave the room a safe and cosy feel. He sat on the sofa opposite hers, his expression still set along grave and serious lines.

'It's incredibly difficult for women and even some men to lose control of their financial affairs. Divorces are messy at the best of times...they don't have to be, but when there's money and assets to divvy up it can be shocking what lengths people will go to. That's why a prenuptial agreement can make things so much more straightforward.'

'But when people fall in love they believe the best of the other person. It can sound so unromantic, even distrustful, to ask for a prenup. It's like saying, *I love you but this is just in case you or I fall out of love some time in the future*.' Aerin screwed up her lips in a self-deprecating smile. 'Sorry, I must sound so naïve and trusting and hopelessly romantic.'

Drake gave a lopsided smile that sent her heart aflutter. 'Promise me you'll sign a prenup when you do find your Mr Perfect. I'll do it pro bono for you.'

Aerin's own smile faded and she uncrossed

her legs and sighed. 'I'm starting to wonder if such a person exists. I mean, I've always had such high standards about everything. I never do anything by halves. I'm all in or not in at all, which is why I've got to the age of almost thirty and never had sex.'

That one word dropping into the silence sent a wave of heat through her body and a strange energy into the atmosphere, like an audience taking a collective breath, waiting for something important to happen...

'Aerin.' There was a stern quality to his voice. And then he let out a long sigh and sent one of his hands through his hair in an agitated manner. His eyes met hers across the distance between the sofas. His gaze glittered darkly, his brows close together, his lips set in a firm line. But then she noticed a pulse beating in his neck and his jaw working like a miniature hammer was tapping beneath his skin. 'We're both tired and need to go to bed, before we step across a boundary neither of us will view the same way in the morning.'

'I wasn't going to ask you to sleep with me.' Or *was* she? Aerin hardly knew what was going to come out of her mouth next. When she was alone with Drake Cawthorn, her body and her brain misfired, making her want things she hadn't thought she would want under such circumstances. Like more of his touch, his deeply passionate kisses, the stroke and glide of his tongue against hers. The heat that roared between their bodies, the surprisingly erotic heat that threatened to overrule her carefully constructed plan for her life. Her Mr Perfect checklist said nothing about having a short-term fling with a man who had openly declared falling in love was not in his game plan. Ever.

Aerin rose from the sofa and began to clear away the mugs.

'Leave it. I'll tidy up. You go on upstairs. I'll see you in the morning.'

Aerin put the mug back down and straightened, aware of the heat in her cheeks and the burning desire in her body. 'Thanks for what you did tonight. The charade and all. I think we managed to convince them we were the real deal.'

A ghost of a smile came and went on his mouth. 'You're welcome, Goldilocks.'

Drake mechanically cleared up their mugs and then made sure the fire screen was securely in place in front of the fireplace. The fire was still smouldering even though he hadn't put any more fuel on it. But so too, were the flames in his body smouldering like red-hot coals. He was in danger of crossing a line he swore he would never cross. And how ironic that it was in one of his safety houses. Maybe he was the one who should have the locked room and get Aerin to lock him in, so he couldn't be tempted to touch her again.

But he was already in a prison of sorts—the prison of his past.

He had shared more with Aerin than he had shared with anyone. The dark stuff kept leaking out of him as if holes had been bored into the steel of his armour and he didn't know how to plug them back up. He was grateful she hadn't pressed him for more details but he found the more he had revealed, the more he wanted to reveal. The tragic and largely avoidable circumstances of his past were something he carried with him every day of his life.

The survivor guilt was heavy and burdensome but his desire to make the world a better place for other people like his mother and sister drove him to work hard. Impossibly hard at times, but even knowing he had potentially saved some lives didn't undo the heartbreaking damage of the lives he had lost. The lives he wished he could have saved, would have saved if only he had known what his father was capable of. The lives of his mother and sister. The two people who had meant the world to him. Their lives taken brutally by his father, who would have taken his life too, if Drake had been home at the time.

But he hadn't been home and he had to live with the knowledge and guilt that came with that inescapable fact. *He had failed to protect his mother and sister.* It wasn't something he could ever forgive himself for, no matter how many shelters and charities he funded.

CHAPTER SIX

AERIN SLEPT DEEPLY for a couple of hours out of sheer exhaustion. But then she woke around dawn to the sound of Drake's muffled voice crying out in a long and anguished, 'No!'

She threw off the bedcovers and quickly pulled on her wrap to cover her nightgown and made her way to his bedroom further down the corridor. She tapped on the door. 'Drake? Are you okay?' There was no answer other than another groan, as if he was in some sort of anguished pain. Was he having some sort of medical event? She knew he occasionally had tension headaches in the past. But Tom had told her that, not Drake.

Aerin opened the door a crack and peered inside the dimly lit bedroom. She could make out his tall frame in the bed, the bedclothes in a tangle around his waist, revealing his flat stomach and toned abdomen. His upper body was naked, his chest sprinkled with dark hair, the same ink-black as his head. He was thrashing from side to side, his eyes tightly closed, his hands bunched into fists as he clutched at the sheets either side of his thighs. 'No, no, no, no!'

Aerin rushed over and, leaning over him, took him by the upper arms, giving him a gentle shake. 'Drake, wake up. You're having a nightmare.'

His eyes snapped wide open like one of those old-fashioned ventriloquist dolls. He blinked a couple of times and then let out a muttered curse and dragged himself up in a sitting position. He moved so quickly she had no choice but to remove her hands from his upper arms, but not before she'd noted how muscular and toned they were.

'Are you okay? I was so worried about you. I thought you might be having a migraine or something.'

Drake scraped his hand through his already tousled hair, her eyes drawn to the bulge of his biceps as he lifted his arm. 'I'm sorry for scaring you. I haven't had a nightmare in years. Ten at least.'

She was still sitting on the edge of his bed and had no desire to move away just yet. 'Maybe it was because of what we talked about in the car coming here last night. Your family being...' She couldn't bring herself to say the brutal word out loud.

Drake reached for her hand where it was resting on the bed next to his thigh. His fingers were warm and gentle around hers and a shiver scuttled down her spine. His expression was difficult to read in the muted light of a greyish dawn, but she could feel something in his touch that spoke volumes.

'I haven't talked to anyone about what happened since I was a teenager. I hated being that kid. The kid whose father killed his own family.'

Aerin gasped. 'Oh, no...' His father killed his mother and sister? His own father? How on earth had he coped with such an awful event?

He gave her a grim look. 'He would have killed me too if I'd been home at the time, but I stayed at a mate's that night, drinking. Can you believe it? I was rip-roaring drunk at the age of fifteen and had no idea of what my father had planned to do.'

Aerin could feel tears pouring from her eyes and her heart was aching as if it were in a vice. 'Oh, you mustn't blame yourself. You were just a kid doing what a lot of boys that age do.'

His top lip curled in self-disgust. 'Yeah, well, not all of those kids do it because their fathers encouraged them to do it. My father liked me to have a beer or three with him. Then he got me to drink spirits. He told me it would make me loosen up a bit. Not be so uptight all the time. Little did I realise it was his plan to stop me from protecting my mother and sister.'

Some pennies were dropping rather loudly in Aerin's head. She glanced at his crooked nose and the scar on his left eyebrow. 'Is that how you got those? Your broken nose and scar?'

Drake let out a ragged sigh. 'I intervened one night when he was laying into my mother, but I wasn't strong enough to take him on. I should have just called the police, but he threatened to kill our dog if I did.' His throat moved up and down and he added in a tone loaded with sadness, 'He did that anyway a few weeks later. He knew how much I loved that damn dog.'

Aerin was openly crying now, broken sobs coming out no matter how hard she tried to stop them. 'I'm so sorry, so very sorry...'

Drake pulled her into his arms, holding her head against his chest, one of his hands gently stroking the back of her head. 'Hey, don't cry, Goldilocks.' His voice was soft and soothing. 'It was all a long time ago and I've managed to make a life for myself. What happened to my mother and sister should never have happened, but it did, and I could have prevented it if I had trusted my gut. But of course hindsight is a wonderful thing, isn't it?'

Aerin kept her head against his chest, her tears still falling for all he had suffered. 'Is he in prison now? Your father?'

'He's dead. It was a murder-suicide. I can only be thankful I wasn't the one to find them. That was a neighbour who ended up with PTSD.'

She lifted her head off his chest to look at him. 'Oh, Drake, it's just so awful to think of what you've been through. Does Tom know any of this? Or did you swear him to secrecy?'

'He doesn't know. I reinvented myself after the event, I felt compelled to. Cawthorn isn't even my real name. I changed my name by deed poll as soon as I was able to. I didn't want to spend the rest of my life being identified as the tragic kid who lost his entire family. I needed to move on and make my life count for something. To do something, anything, to change things for others like my mother and sister. But the figures on domestic violence are still way too high, not just in the UK but worldwide.'

'But at least you are doing something,' Aerin said. 'You're making a true difference in so many lives. The charity, the safety houses—it's such an honourable thing to do to use your own time and money to bring about change. There's a lot of talk about the issue of domestic violence but not enough action. Of course, any action you take now can never bring your mother and sister back but they would be so proud of you, I'm sure.'

One of Drake's hands was resting on the bed close to her hand. She wasn't sure whose hand moved first but suddenly his fingers and hers were entwined. Their gazes met and the air hummed with an electric energy.

'I think kissing you must've unlocked something in my psyche,' he said, slowly stroking his thumb over the fleshy part of her thumb. 'I still haven't figured out if that is a good thing or a bad thing.'

Aerin's eyes flicked to his mouth and her heart gave a little skip. 'Kissing you has unlocked something in me too.' It had awakened her to full-blooded human desire, the physical urge so strong and insistent she couldn't imagine having her first time with anyone else but him. He was the first man to kiss her. Why not ask him to be her first lover? It might help her overcome her cycle of perfectionistic procrastination. How else could she jump-start her life unless she took some decisive action? Don't wait for it to happen. *Make* it happen. That would be her new mantra.

A dark intensity shone in his eyes as they held hers. His thumb strokes on her hand were mesmerisingly slow and sensual, sending waves of incendiary heat throughout her body.

'This…chemistry we have is not something we have to act on,' Drake said in a husky tone.

'But what if I did want to act on it? Just until we get back to London?'

His thumb stopped stroking hers and a frown was etched on his forehead in twin pleats between his eyes. 'You're not talking sense, Aerin. Nothing of that nature can happen between us. You know it can't.'

'Because I'm a virgin?'

He drew in a deep breath and released it in a rush. 'That and because you're someone I can't just walk away from and never think of again.'

'No one has to know we've slept together. You're obviously good at keeping secrets, this one won't be hard to keep, surely?'

Drake suddenly pushed back the bedcovers and rolled out of the bed on the opposite side to where she was sitting. He stood and then strode over to the windows and pulled back the curtains with an almost savage movement of his hand. He stood with his back to her, staring at the view outside. The light that poured in was so pallid, it barely made any difference to the room. But it was enough light to see his physical perfection.

She found it hard to take her eyes off his tall and athletic form, her gaze drawn by sheer magnetic force. Broad shoulders and a strong back tapering to a lean waist and slim hips, his only article of clothing a pair of black satin boxer shorts. The muscles of his long legs toned from hard exercise. An olive-toned tan covered his body and gave his skin a glow that made it all the more tempting for her to touch him.

Drake turned to look at her, his expression grave. 'We have a problem.'

Aerin was conscious of the heat flooding into her cheeks. She had made a spectacular fool of herself, coming across as gauche and unsophisticated, practically begging him to make love to her when he clearly wasn't interested. She rose from where she was perched on the edge of the bed with a sigh. 'Save me the lecture. I get it. You don't want to sleep with me. Sorry for embarrassing you by asking you.'

'I'm not embarrassed. But that's not the problem I'm talking about right now. Look.'

He pulled back the curtains a little further and she walked over to where he was standing and peered out of the windows. Snow had fallen overnight and it now covered everything in a white blanket as magical as a fairyland setting. The blue spruce pines were shrouded, some of the lower limbs bowing with the weight of snow, and the wide expanse of lawn was now a rectangle of white unmarked by any footprints, either animal or human.

'Oh, wow, snow!' Aerin said, unable to tone down the excitement of seeing it for the first time since last winter. 'Isn't it beautiful?'

Drake was standing right next to her, so close she could feel the brush of his upper arm against her left shoulder. 'Let me guess. Number Nine on your Mr Perfect checklist is *Must love snow*?'

Aerin turned to look up at him. He had a sardonic smile on his face that should have annoyed her but somehow didn't. She was getting to know and understand what was behind his mocking and cynical façade. 'Actually, I don't have a Number Nine or Ten. My list only goes to Eight.'

His gaze went to her mouth and it seemed to take him quite some effort to lift it again to meet her eyes. 'Aerin…' He swallowed deeply and continued, 'The car we drove up in is not an all-terrain vehicle.'

'So?'

'So, snow.'

Aerin frowned. 'You mean we can't leave? It's not safe on the roads?'

'Not until the snow melts a bit.' He glanced back out of the window. 'It looks like we might be in for another decent fall. See those clouds over there? I should've checked the weather app before I brought you here. And I should've booked a different vehicle.' The bitter self-recrimination in his voice was unmistakable.

'Because, clearly, being snowbound with me in a cottage in Scotland is your worst nightmare.' Aerin found it hard to remove the bitter edge to her own voice. Did he have to make her feel any more hideously embarrassed about herself? He'd probably had dozens of snowbound weekends with his long list of casual lovers, but he was baulking at the thought of one with her. Was she so undesirable? His kisses hadn't given her that impression at all, but rather the opposite.

'My worst nightmare happened twenty-one years ago, so no, being snowbound with you is not in the same category at all.'

Aerin bit down on her lower lip and cast him an apologetic glance. 'I'm sorry. My choice of words was a little insensitive.'

He lifted his hand to her face and glided one finger down from the top of her cheekbone to the base of her chin in a faineant movement that sent a shower of sparks down her spine. 'But it's still a problem.'

She ran the point of her tongue over her suddenly paper-dry lips. 'Why?' Her voice came out whisper soft.

His gaze drifted to her mouth and her heart rate sped up. His lazy finger left her face and traced the contour of her mouth, sending ticklish tingles through her flesh. 'Because I want to do this so damn much it hurts.' His mouth came down and covered hers in a gentle kiss that throbbed with reined in erotic energy.

Aerin instinctively moved closer to him, her hands sliding up his chest to then link around his neck. Drake gave a low deep groan and put one of his hands in the small of her back, pressing her to his hardening body. His tongue commanded entry to her mouth and she welcomed him in with a breathless sigh of pleasure. The playful duelling of his tongue with hers sent liquid heat to her core, making her legs tremble with growing need.

His other hand came down to rest on her hip, his touch electrifying even through the layers of her nightgown and wrap. His kiss deepened, became more passionate, more desperate. Never had she dreamed a kiss could incite such fiery lust in her body. Never had she imagined a man's lips and tongue could stir her senses into freefall. It was as though she had waited all her life for this moment—this passionate awakening of the senses that made her ache in her feminine core.

Drake lifted his mouth off hers but still kept her in his embrace. 'I want to touch you.' His voice was a deep, rough burr that sounded as if it were coming from Middle-earth itself.

'Then touch me.' Excitement thrummed in her blood, her heart hammered, her pulse raced, desire flaring between her legs in a tight throbbing ache.

His hand came up from her hip and gently

brushed against her breast through the satin of her wrap and nightgown. It was a barely touching caress and yet it sent a laser strike of lust through her body. She pressed herself closer and his hand touched her breast again, this time cupping it in his hand. Aerin let out a gasp of pleasure, hardly believing it was possible that her breast could feel so different when touched by him instead of herself.

'Touch me skin on skin.'

'Are you sure?'

'I'm sure.' She hadn't been surer of anything in her entire life. His touch was what she wanted. What she craved. It was as if she had been waiting all this time for this to happen—for Drake to be the one to introduce her to the wonderland of sensuality. She couldn't explain why she was so driven to allow him to be the first one to make love to her. It didn't make sense in the light of her checklist and careful plans for her life. But right now, it was the only thing she wanted. She was living in the moment in a way she had never done before. Not thinking too far ahead, just rolling with the tide of want that consumed her so totally.

Drake eased aside her nightgown and

cupped her naked breast, his eyes gleaming. 'You're so perfect.'

Body issues were the bane of many young women's lives and while she was mostly happy with what genetics had handed her, there were some things she was self-conscious about. She had never been naked in front of a man before. She'd thought she would feel embarrassed, but she didn't. It seemed the most natural thing in the world to reveal her body to Drake, to have his eyes devour her form.

'I'm a bit on the small side…'

'Nonsense. You're just right. Not too big, not too small.' He stroked the pad of his thumb across her budded nipple and a tingle of delight went through her breast. Then he circled her nipple with one of his fingers, his touch light and explorative as if he was committing her shape to memory. His head came down and he caressed her breast with his lips and tongue, the tingling sensations flowing through her like a hot current.

Aerin could feel the proud ridge of his erection pressing against her, making her need for him all the more out of control. Who knew this alchemy could happen between two people? This ferocious need to be skin on skin, to touch and be touched, to desire and be desired. It was mysterious and magical and she wanted to experience all of it. Every step and stage of lust, the steps and stages she had only ever experienced in solo and in secret. To experience it with someone she admired and felt safe and comfortable with was surely the right thing to do at this point in her life. She could not turn thirty without having experienced making love with someone she desired.

Drake came back to kiss her on the lips once more, as if drawn there by a force beyond his control. His tongue thrust between her lips and it sent a shock wave of delight through her, the flickering movement of his tongue stoking a roaring fire in her loins. He lifted his mouth off hers and sent it on a blazing trail down the side of her neck, gently moving aside her nightgown as he went. He kissed and caressed her other breast, his lips and tongue working their magic on her naked flesh until she was all but purring with pleasure.

'You like that?'

'How could I not? You seem to know exactly what to do to make me want you all the more.' Aerin gave him a twisted smile. 'But then, you've had a lot of experience.'

Drake placed his hands on her hips, holding her to him but lightly enough to give her the freedom to move away if she wanted to. 'I admit I've lost count of how many lovers I've had, mostly because in the early days I used sex to blank out a lot of other stuff.' He let out a sigh and continued, 'I don't want to give you the impression I use women as sexual objects. Not these days, at least. I only sleep with women who want the same as me—casual and uncomplicated sex, which is why going any further with you is wrong on so many counts.'

'But how is it wrong if I want that too?'

'It's wrong because I can't give you more than a fling.'

This was probably not the time to point out to Drake that Lucas Rothwell and Jack Livingstone had said much the same words to Ruby and Harper and yet they were all happily together now. Dared she hope the same could happen to her? That Drake would gradually lower his guard and fall in love with her as Lucas and Jack had fallen for her friends?

Aerin placed her hands on the strong wall of his chest, looking up at him with clear focus. 'What if we were to forget about my checklist and the fact that you only ever do flings? What if we just went with the flow while we're stuck here?'

Drake's gaze drifted to her upturned mouth and his hands shifted from her hips to her waist. Then his narrowed gaze came back to hers. 'Is this a pity thing?'

Aerin closed her eyes in a slow blink to quell her frustration. Couldn't he see how much she wanted him? It wasn't about his tragic past but about *him*. The essential Drake she was finding so hard to resist. 'No, it's nothing to do with pity. Of course I feel sorry you've had such a shocking thing happen to you. But I want you for you. I want you to be my first lover. I don't want to get to the age of thirty and still be a virgin. I think you're the right person to give me that experience because I know and trust you. I'm not asking for anything other than a weekend fling.'

Drake released her from his light hold and

put a slight distance between them. There was a battle playing out over his features, a tug-of-war between his body wanting to do as she suggested and his mind carefully weighing up the dangers. Muscles tensed in his jaw, shadows came and went in his gaze, the strong column of his throat rose and fell in a tight swallow. 'Are you sure you can keep your emotions out of it?' he asked, still frowning.

'I don't know because I've never slept with anyone before.' But weren't her emotions already in it now? Feelings she was trying to keep hidden. Feelings that had bloomed into life ever since his first kiss, like a spring bulb poking its head from beneath the ground, thawed by the warming rays of spring sunshine. 'How do you keep *your* emotions out of it?'

He gave a crooked smile that didn't make it to his eyes. His eyes were still troubled, the shadows lurking, the doubts circling, the yes and no debate ongoing. 'It's never been a problem before.'

Aerin closed the distance between them and lifted her hand to his unshaven jaw. 'But you're worried it might become one with me?' She stroked her fingers along the stubble-roughened skin, a light shiver coursing over her own flesh.

His strong hand encircled her wrist in a firm but gentle hold, his eyes locking on hers. 'It's a possibility that does concern me.'

Wasn't that something positive to cling to? That he was prepared to admit he could be in danger of falling for her? Didn't that show he had the potential to love even though he claimed he didn't? He lifted her wrist and turned it over to place a kiss to the sensitive skin on the underside. She shivered again, his electrifying touch sending livewires of need to her core.

'Because you don't want to hurt me or get hurt yourself?' she asked.

Drake planted another feather-light kiss to her wrist, the slight graze of his stubble against her skin sending a wave of incendiary heat and rolling fire through her blood. 'Some people don't care if they hurt others. But I do.'

He hadn't fully answered her question, though, about whether he was worried about getting hurt himself. Or had he already endured a lifetime's quota of hurt and pain?

Losing his family in such a horrendous way was certainly a harrowing experience that would leave deep emotional scars.

Aerin ran her fingers through the thickness of his dark hair, her body so close to his she could feel her softer contours melting into his harder ones. Her breasts against his chest, her pelvis in the cradle of his hips, her thighs against his muscular ones...and the potent rise of his male body against her most sensitive flesh of all. 'If I wasn't a virgin, would you be feeling a little less reluctant, do you think?'

Drake slipped an arm around her back and brought her even closer, his bottomless brown eyes burning with lust. His other hand went to the back of her head, his fingers splaying through her hair, sending hot tingles down her spine. 'Physically, as you can probably tell, I'm not at all reluctant. But this is not going to be something we can forget ever happened. I'll always be your first lover, the first man who kissed you. And you'll be the first woman I've slept with who I can't simply delete from my phone and forget about. I don't want you to be embarrassed or uncomfortable when we cross paths in the future, either at one of your family's gatherings or professionally.'

'We've both adults, Drake. You're making it sound so terribly complicated. All I want is this weekend. Once it's over, we can pretend it never happened and move on with our lives.'

His eyes softened and he brushed a stray hair away from her face, a lopsided smile on his mouth. 'I have a feeling I'm not going to forget about it in a hurry.' He drew in a deep breath and released it in a not quite steady stream.

Aerin lifted her hand to his face and stroked his lean jaw. 'Nor me.'

His head came down and his mouth closed over hers in a searing kiss that sent a riot of sensations through her body. His tongue didn't ask for entry but demanded it, tangling with hers in a sexy combat that mimicked the intimacy they both craved. This was not a chaste kiss between old friends. This was not a kiss that could ever be forgotten. This was a kiss of urgency and explosive heat and longing. Drake's mouth continued its thrilling exploration of hers while his hands slipped beneath the opening of her wrap. She shivered as his hand shaped her, his caresses threatening to heat her blood to boiling.

Until he had touched her, she'd had no idea her breasts were so sensitive. She had not realised the intensity of feeling to have a man's hand cradle her shape while his thumb moved back and forth across her engorged nipple. But she wanted more than his hands on her breasts and, as if he had read her mind, he bent his head and took her nipple into the warm cave of his mouth. Aerin arched her spine as the tingling sensations shot through her, a groan of pleasure escaping her lips. 'That feels…so…so…good…'

Drake went to her other breast, exploring it in the same erotic detail, his lips and tongue wreaking havoc on her senses. But it wasn't enough. She wanted more. More skin-on-skin contact, more friction. More of the sensual heat his body promised as it surged against her.

Drake lifted his mouth from her breast and captured her mouth again in a kiss that was even more thrilling. His tongue played with hers in a game of catch-me-if-you-can and her heart pounded with excitement.

His hands skimmed down the sides of her body, up and down in a caressing motion that made her skin lift in a delicate shiver. He peeled her wrap away from her body, his mouth still clamped to hers. But then he pulled back and, breathing heavily, slowly, ever so slowly peeled away her nightgown until it fell in a pool of satin at her feet. His eyes roved over her body, his gaze shining with lust as he took in every inch of her naked form.

'You're so damn beautiful…' There was a note of wonder in his tone as if he had never seen a woman quite like her before. But then, maybe he hadn't. She was hardly his usual type with her understated girl-next-door looks.

Aerin glanced down at the shape of him tenting his black boxer shorts. She was too shy to touch him but ached to do so. He took her hand and held it against his swollen flesh, allowing her to feel him through the satin.

'Don't be afraid to touch me,' he said in a husky tone.

Her fingers stroked the turgid length of him and, with a boldness she'd had no idea she possessed, she slipped her hand beneath the satin and touched him skin on skin. He shuddered and groaned, his face contorting with pleasure.

'I think you're going to be a quick learner,' he said with a gleam in his eyes. Then he scooped her up in his arms like a hero out of an old black and white movie from the golden days of Hollywood and carried her to his bed…

Drake knew he could have put a stop to things right then and there but for once in his life he couldn't access his willpower. He wanted Aerin as he had wanted no other woman. He had weighed up the pros and cons of engaging in a weekend fling with her, he had carefully measured the risks and done his checks and balances. The rational part of his brain told him to keep his distance but another part of his brain—or maybe it wasn't his brain at all but his body alone—told him to have this secret weekend with her. To have what he had wanted from the moment he saw her across the street from his office. Their first kiss had only reinforced the want, the driving need, the urge he couldn't dampen down no matter how much he tried.

But was he worrying *too* much? Aerin was looking for the fairy tale, the perfect partner and he was certainly not that. She had already ruled him out with her eight-point checklist. She wouldn't allow herself to fall in love with anyone less than perfect, so why shouldn't he indulge her wish for a fling?

Drake laid her on his rumpled bed and stood above her for a long moment, hungrily taking in the slim curves of her body. She was so lithe and lissom, her skin a pale cream without a single blemish. Her golden blonde hair was tousled around her shoulders and he couldn't wait to bury his head in it and breathe in its flowery scent.

A worried look came into Aerin's eyes. 'Are you having second thoughts?'

He kneeled one knee on the bed beside her and leaned forward to cage her in with his arms. 'Are you?'

'No.' She lifted her hand to his nearest shoulder and stroked her fingers down the length of his arm in a touch as light as fairy footsteps. 'I want you.'

'You know this is madness, don't you? Us doing this.'

Her other hand trailed down his other arm, sending shivers up and down his spine. Her gaze was luminous at it met his, shining with the same need he knew shone in his. 'It would be madness if we both didn't agree on the terms.'

Drake planted a kiss on her lips, a long passionate kiss that sent his blood pounding all the more. He was hard and aching to possess her but he knew he would have to slow down and take things gently with her. She had cast some sort of spell over him, a magical spell that made it impossible for him to walk away and leave her well alone.

He straightened from the bed to step out of his boxer shorts. 'I have to get a condom.'

'Do you have any with you?'

'I always carry some in my wallet.'

She chewed at her lower lip for a moment, her eyes downcast. 'Of course...'

Drake picked up his wallet from where he had left it on the bedside table. But then he snapped its folds back together. 'It's too late to change your mind.'

'Why would I change my mind?'

He took in her pink cheeks and unblinking grey-blue gaze.

'Because I'm a playboy and you're a virgin.'

Her cheeks darkened another shade but her eyes remained steady on his. 'I'm not making any judgements on your lifestyle. You're not currently seeing anyone, so I don't see a problem.'

Drake could see a problem. His past was a problem that cast long shadows over his life. How he could be sure those dark shadows wouldn't somehow taint Aerin by being closer to him than anyone had got in years? He had told her things he had told no one. She had not pressed or pushed him to reveal his childhood trauma but he had opened up to her all the same. Why had he allowed her to get past the fortress he had built around his emotional centre? Wouldn't making love to her only bring her closer?

He would be her first lover.

That was not something he could dismiss from his mind like so many of his other lovers who had faded so easily into the background. He would carry the memory of this experience with Aerin for the rest of his life.

And so would she of him. He would not be able to look at her without seeing her like this—naked, hungry for him, her chin reddened by his stubble. She would not be able to look at him and not recall this stolen moment of pleasure. What if he hurt her, even unintentionally? Could he live with that? Could he live with more guilt to lug around?

But maybe guilt was the price to pay for what he wanted right now.

Drake came back over to her and tilted her face up so her gaze meshed with his. His brushed his thumb across the reddened circle on her chin. 'I've given you beard rash.'

'Have you?'

He bent his head and lightly kissed her chin. 'I should shave before I make love to you.'

Her hand came up and stroked the rough stubble on his jaw. 'I like the feel of it, so raspy and prickly.'

Drake stroked her smooth cheek with a lazy finger. 'Your first time might be a little uncomfortable. I'll take it slowly and make sure you're well prepared.'

'Isn't that a bit of a myth? That all virgins feel discomfort or bleed? I read an article about it somewhere. Being forced to prove one's virginity is an outdated patriarchal practice that still happens in some developing countries. I've been physically active all my life so I might not feel a thing.'

He slipped his hands down to her waist, his smile wry. 'I'll definitely have to work on my technique if you don't feel a thing when we make love.'

Her cheeks were tinged with pink but her eyes were alight with anticipation. Her arms came up and looped around his neck, her breasts pressed against his chest, stirring his blood to a roaring, rushing river of fire. 'I thought I'd be nervous but I'm not with you. This feels like it's meant to be. Does that make sense?'

Drake brushed an imaginary wisp of hair off her face. 'It makes perfect sense,' he said, and, joining her on the bed, brought his mouth down to hers.

Because in a weird sort of way it did make sense. They were snowbound, secluded, and attracted to each other. Why not enjoy this for what it was? A secret weekend fling that would be over before it got a chance to do any permanent damage.

CHAPTER SEVEN

AERIN SIGHED WITH deep pleasure as Drake's tongue tangled with hers in a sexy salsa. Her pulse rate soared, her lower body melting as the molten heat of desire flowed through her. Her hands explored him with increasing boldness, her fingers rolling over the tiny pebbles of his nipples and gliding over the toned muscles of his chest, the washboard ridges of his abdomen marking him as a man who enjoyed hard exercise.

She shuddered as his hand glided up her body to just below her breast. The warmth of his hand against her ribcage so close to the sensitive flesh of her breast drove her wild with anticipation. He brought his mouth to the upper curve of her breast, his tongue circling her pert nipple, her senses reeling at the expertise of his caress. He suckled on her gently, drawing her nipple into the warmth of his mouth, then slowly releasing it. He did the same to her other breast, sending shivers down her spine as his lips and tongue explored her contours in intimate detail.

He moved from her breasts to kiss a pathway to her belly button. 'Relax for me.' His voice was deep and husky and his warm breath caressed the skin of her stomach.

She lay back and gripped the bedcovers either side of her body. 'I'm trying to...'

He glanced up at her, leaning his weight on one elbow. 'I won't do anything you don't want to do. Tell me to stop if you're not comfortable.'

Aerin let out a shuddering breath. 'Okay.'

Drake kissed her stomach again, then slowly worked his way down to the juncture of her thighs. Her female flesh was already swelling and twitching in excitement, pulses of lust firing through her like a current. He stroked her with his fingers, long slow strokes that sent her blood skyrocketing through her veins. The liquid heat intensified and the ache of need building in her core rose to an unbearable level.

Drake brought his mouth down to her most intimate flesh and the rhythmic strokes of his tongue sent a torrent of tingles through her body, concentrating in that one exquisite point—the heart of her femininity. The tension grew to a crescendo until she was finally catapulted into a spinning vortex that scattered her thoughts, leaving her without the ability to think, only to feel. And feel she did. Giant waves of pleasure unlike anything she had experienced when going solo. Showers of goosebumps peppered her body, she was dazed and limbless and out of her mind as the aftershocks rippled through her.

'*Oh...*' A breathless gasp escaped her lips and she opened her eyes to find Drake looking at her indulgently.

'Good?'

Aerin let out a long blissful sigh, still trying to grasp how her body had responded to his intimate caresses. 'I'm not sure I have the words to describe it.'

Drake stroked a gentle hand down the flank of her thigh, sending another ripple of pleasure through her body. His eyes were impossibly dark, his pupils flared wide with lust. Her hand reached for him, stroking his potent length with shy fingers at first but she was emboldened by the expression on his

face signalling his growing delight. He drew
in a harsh breath and pulled her hand away.

'I need to put on a condom before we go
any further.'

Aerin knew protection should always be a
priority unless a couple was actively seeking
to conceive. But something about Drake's
tone reminded her that kids were something
he never wanted in his life. She understood
why, given the bleak circumstances of his
own childhood, but it still made her sad
that he had permanently ruled out one of
the things most important to her. She could
not imagine a future without a family. She
had grown up in a loving home and had been
sheltered and nurtured by parents who loved
her and her brother as well as each other.
That was what she wanted for her life.

Aerin leaned up on her elbows to watch
him apply the condom. 'How many do you
have stashed away in your wallet?'

He glanced at her with a twinkling look.
'Enough.'

'Three? Four? More?'

He came back over to her and pressed a
long drugging kiss to her lips. He lifted his

mouth off hers and looked deeply into her eyes. 'Enough to get us through the weekend.'

'What if the snow doesn't melt in time?'

His eyes flicked to her mouth and then back to her gaze, a shadow passing through his before he disguised it behind a playful smile. 'I'll have to get some airlifted in.'

Aerin's brows shot up in surprise. 'You can do that?'

He leaned down and kissed the tip of her nose. 'You bet I can.'

His mouth covered hers again and sent her pulses racing. His aroused body was pressing against her thigh and it ramped up her need for him all the more. To know it was her who had made him so turned on thrilled her. It gave her a sense of power she had never experienced before.

The kiss deepened, became more urgent, their limbs tangling with an erotic choreography as if they had made love in another lifetime. The alignment of their limbs for that ultimate moment of physical connection was simple and yet complex. Natural and yet strange. It was like learning the steps of a dance, one leg this way, the other that way, one arm here, the other there. Their chests close, their hips even closer. There was no shyness or hesitancy on Aerin's part. It felt completely normal to be in bed with Drake Cawthorn, his mouth clamped to hers, his hands caressing her breasts with exquisite tenderness. He made some guttural noises as her hands continued to explore him. Deep masculine sounds that spoke of a man who was keeping himself on a tight leash of self-control.

Drake dragged his mouth off hers, his breathing heavy. 'I want to be inside you, but I don't want to rush you.'

She lifted a hand to his hair, brushing it further back from his forehead. 'I'm ready for you. I want you.'

'Are you sure?'

'Of course I'm sure.' And she was. Right now, this was all she wanted. She refused to think about her checklist...about all the points on it Drake didn't tick. Wouldn't tick. Couldn't tick. Maybe she had been a bit too pedantic constructing a checklist in the first place. Maybe the Mr Perfect she longed for might never come along. She might have to learn to settle on something a little less than perfect even if it jarred with her perfection-istic outlook on life.

But nothing about Drake's lovemaking was less than perfect.

Her body sang arias under his touch. Her flesh tingled from head to foot and her senses did cartwheels of delight.

Drake gently probed her entrance, allow-ing her time to get used to him just being there. Close enough for her to feel the heft and weight of him without overwhelming her.

Aerin stroked his back and shoulders, loving the feel of him against her, his bulk against her slim build a heady reminder of all that was different between them.

He slowly entered her, waiting for her to relax before he went any further. 'Are you okay with this?'

'Perfectly...' A shiver coursed over her as her intimate muscles began to stretch to take hold of him.

He began a slow rhythm that sent plea-sure rippling through her body, the friction of male against female making her aware of her body in a way she had never been before. Nerves she'd had no idea were so intricately laced into her body were firing up, fizzing with life and sensual energy. Muscles that had been inactive for most of her life were now being subjected to a deeply pleasurable workout that had one sure goal. She could feel the anticipation of it beating in her blood. A tribal, primitive drumbeat that throbbed with increasing urgency.

'You feel so damn good,' Drake groaned against her mouth.

'So do you,' Aerin said, sweeping her tongue over his lower lip.

He thrust a little faster, a little deeper, his breathing as hectic as hers. A restless ache was building in her female flesh, a low dragging ache that was almost unbearable.

But as if Drake could read her silent pleas for more of that delicious friction, he slipped his hand between their bodies and sought the tightly budded heart of her arousal. The feminine bud of nerves that spread from that tightened point all throughout her pelvis. The stroking of his fingers against her slick wetness, with his own body tightly encased inside hers, sent her into a freefall of spinning, whirling, dizzying sensations. They ricocheted through her in giant shudders, making her lose her grasp on conscious thought. So *this* was mind-blowing sex. Sending her to a place almost beyond consciousness. Fireworks went off in her head, in her blood, the vivid colours bursting behind her squeezed-shut eyelids as she rode out the waves.

Then there was the slow wash of a wave of lassitude…like the tide finally quietening after a ferocious storm at sea.

But then, Aerin could feel another storm building, not in her flesh but in Drake's. His thrusts becoming more urgent, more desperate, his breathing laboured, as if his control were hanging by a gossamer thread. She could feel the exact moment he let go through the silky walls of her feminine flesh. The pitching forward of his bulk, the ecstatic groan forced from him as powerfully as the life essence from his body. Something about that primal groan and those deep shudders of his sent a shiver across the floor of her belly like a breeze whispering over a lake. They were still joined intimately, their bodies in a tangle of limbs that made her feel safe and protected.

Drake's hand stroked the hair away from

her face, his gaze searching. 'How are you feeling?' There was a chord of concern in the lower pitch of his voice, the same concern she could feel in his touch.

'I feel...wonderful. You didn't hurt me at all. It was amazing.' Aerin didn't have the words to truly express how he had made her feel. But would he want to hear them in any case? He was used to casual encounters that probably didn't include discussing how mind-blowing the sex was. She was supposed to be keeping her feelings out of this. Feelings were not a part of their weekend fling. Feelings were not a part of any of his encounters. They were not a part of his life...and yet she wondered if one day he would allow them to be. He had so much to offer. He was kind and gentle and far more sensitive than she had given him credit for in the past. Behind his cynical façade was a wounded man who cared deeply but was guarded about showing it.

Drake continued to look at her unwaveringly. 'No regrets?'

Her only regret was he was not interested in anything more than a weekend fling. Making love with him once or twice was not going to be enough. He had awakened a hunger in her that was not going to be so easily satisfied. It was tasting an exotic fruit for the first time and wanting more. 'Not so far.' She painted a smile on her face. 'You?'

He drew in a deep breath and released it on a rough-edged sigh. 'Only that this feels a little strange.'

'How so?'

He played with a wisp of her hair, winding it around his finger and letting it go again, the soft tug against her scalp sending a shiver rolling down her spine. 'Being with you like this.'

'No one has to know about it but us.'

A frown pulled at his brow. 'You won't even tell Ruby and Harper?'

Aerin ran the tip of her tongue over her lips. That was certainly going to be a little trickier to navigate than the reunion charade. That had worked on her school friends because she saw them so infrequently, but she worked closely with Harper and Ruby. They saw each other most days and even on weekends when they had a wedding. They knew her better than anyone. How was she going to conceal this from them? Could she conceal it or would it show on her person somehow?

Making love with Drake had been the most incredible experience of her life. She *felt* different, not just physically but—even more worryingly—emotionally. Everyone said you never forgot your first lover and there could be both good and bad reasons for that. But how much harder to forget when that first lover was so tender and attentive and made your pleasure and comfort paramount? How could she not fall a little bit in love with him?

'If you'd rather I didn't, then I won't. But I have to warn you they know me so well that they're likely to sense something's happened.'

Drake rolled away to dispose of the condom, then he came back to her, one of his hands capturing one of hers. His thumb stroked the back of her hand in a slow-moving caress that was soothing and yet hotly sensual at the same time. 'There's this saying I read somewhere, how you can ruin a perfectly good friendship by bringing sex into the equation.'

'But we weren't particularly friends in the first place, were we?'

He gave a half-smile. 'I guess not. You always seemed intent on avoiding me whenever you could. Tom even asked me a few months back if I'd done something to upset you.'

Aerin gave a shame-faced grimace. 'I was always so prejudiced against you. Your cynicism was so jarring up against my optimism and plan for lifelong love. I'm sorry I didn't take the time to get to know you better.'

Drake tucked a strand of her hair behind one of her ears, his touch so tender it made her heart squeeze as if it were in a vice. A flicker of something moved through his gaze like a passing thought leaving a long shadow in its wake. 'Are you sure I didn't hurt you when we made love?'

'I'm totally sure.'

His eyes drifted to her mouth and her pulse picked up its pace. 'I have this compulsive desire to kiss you again.'

Aerin linked her arms around his neck. She had a compulsion of her own—to feel his arms around her, to feel his body move within her, to feel the magic of his lovemaking all over again. 'Feel free.'

Drake rested his forehead on hers, his warm breath mingling with hers. 'Are you sure you wouldn't rather go outside and build a snowman or something?' There was a playful note in his voice.

Aerin toyed with the thick strands of his hair at the back of his head, her gaze mesmerised by the glint in his. 'Not right now. Or do you have a burning desire to make one before we even have breakfast?'

He smiled and a wave of heat coursed through her. 'I only have a burning desire for you.' And his mouth came down and proved it beyond a doubt.

Drake had lost count of the number of lovers he had had over the years, but he knew he would never forget this weekend with Aerin. How could he forget the sweet suppleness of her mouth? The soft shy touch of her hands on his naked skin? Her flowery fragrance that clung to his skin and dazzled his senses? The warm, wet, silky welcome of her body?

He was her first lover.

He couldn't get that sentence, that inescapable *fact* out of his mind. Nothing could ever be the same between them after this weekend. He was fooling himself to think it could. He had no intention of letting anyone know about their fling, but he was concerned others would find out, such as Aerin's friends. Or perhaps, her school friends would let something slip out on social media in spite of their promises not to. He didn't want their fling to be gossip fodder. He loathed sensationalised journalism. He had suffered enough of that when his father destroyed his family. Drake had seen headlines and stories no fifteen-year-old kid should ever see, especially when it was his family that was referenced there. It was one of the reasons he changed his surname. He couldn't bear the thought of anyone doing a search on him and reading about the worst event of his life.

But when he kissed Aerin, all of the dark shadows of his past melted away. She woke something in him that had been in a long cold hibernation. He could feel the tentative stirring in his chest, like the cramped limbs of a faceless creature slowly unfolding. He could feel the sense of freedom flowing through him, a sense of space he had not allowed himself in years.

The space to breathe.

The space to feel.

To *really* feel.

The soft but urgent press of Aerin's lips against his made his blood pound in his veins. The touch of her hands made every nerve beneath his skin come to throbbing life. Her taste was sweet and yet exotic, forbidden and yet addictive in a way he had no power to resist. Where was his damn willpower? The iron-strong willpower that had made him steer clear of intimate relationships where emotions clouded everything?

He had not intended to sleep with her this weekend. Of course the thought had crossed his mind but he hadn't allowed it to get too comfortable in there. But since making love with her, now other thoughts were not only crossing his mind but finding a seat to lounge in, order coffee and cake and stay put. Thoughts of not just one weekend with Aerin but a few weeks, a month or two, maybe more. Thoughts of what it would be like to be open to everyone about their relationship, instead of covering it up like a dirty little secret.

He didn't want to make Aerin feel he was ashamed to be with her. He wasn't…but he was conflicted. It was as if there were suddenly two men inside him caught in a vicious tug of war. One wanted to keep safe inside the fortress, madly locking all the points of exit, while the other was sliding the bolts back, taking the fortress down brick by brick, nail by nail.

Drake was the man who didn't do relationships. He was the no strings, no rings, no promises guy who lived his life as a playboy. But kissing Aerin had changed him, transformed him like in one of those old fairy tales. The frog had turned into a prince who wanted to get out of the murky pond he'd been condemned to and live in the real world. The world of love and happiness and hope.

But did that world even exist? Especially for someone like him?

CHAPTER EIGHT

AERIN MUST HAVE drifted off to sleep after making love the second time, for when she woke, she saw Drake looking down at her with a contemplative look on his face. One of his hands was idly stroking the bare skin of her arm, a soft almost ticklish caress that sent shivers of delight down her spine.

She stretched her limbs and encountered one of his hairy legs. The sheer intimacy of lying in bed with him, let alone what had happened between them during their passionate lovemaking session, was mind-blowing. She was acutely, intensely, spine-tinglingly aware of him. The dark glitter in his eyes, the shape of his mouth that had given such pleasure out of her. The lean jaw with its generous regrowth of dark stubble, the strong column of his neck, his broad shoulders. Shoulders that had carried for too long a heavy burden from his past. A past he had spoken only to her about in such detail.

Did that mean he had a special place for her in his life? In his heart? Or was she being a fool to think he would ever lower his guard enough to fall in love? He made love to her so exquisitely it was impossible to imagine he didn't feel something for her. But then, she reminded herself, he was an experienced playboy. He had made love to dozens of women. She was just another in a long line of conquests.

And yet, she didn't see herself as a conquest. He had certainly never made her feel that way. Besides, she had been the one to instigate their intimacy. He had made her feel in control from the get-go. And yet her body had been out of control the moment he kissed her. She had no resistance to him, no immunity to the potency of his touch.

'Sleeping Beauty awakes,' Drake said with a teasing smile.

Aerin smiled back. 'Hey, thought I was Goldilocks?'

He released a little puff of air that was part laugh, part something else. 'Yes, well, you want everything just right.' He picked up a fistful of her hair and trailed it through his fingertips and added, 'And your hair is like spun gold.'

She rested her hand on his chest, right over the steady *thud-thud-thud* of his heart. 'I've always been a perfectionist—just ask my parents and Tom.' She gave a soft sigh and continued, 'I'm not sure it's doing me any favours, though. I mean, it's great for my work and all but not so good for my personal life. I think it's held me back. The fear of making a mistake has made me stall in some areas of my life.'

There was a long moment of silence. The only sound was the rustling of the bedsheets when Drake moved one of his legs.

'Do you consider what happened between us this weekend a mistake?' There was a sombre quality to his voice, a slight rumble of uncertainty she hadn't heard in it before.

Aerin forced her gaze back to his. 'No. Do you?'

One side of his mouth came up in a rueful slant and his hand continued its slow stroke of her forearm. 'Yes and no.'

Her heart sank like a pricked balloon. Did he regret making love to her? Had she disappointed him in some way? Was he disgusted with himself for crossing the line he had sworn he would never cross? She disguised a nervous swallow. 'I'm sorry if I've made you feel compromised. You didn't have to make love to me. You could have said no.'

His gaze darkened and his hand came up to cup her cheek. 'Saying no to you wasn't as easy as I imagined it would be.' He leaned down and pressed a soft-as-air kiss to her lips. 'This is all it took—one kiss.'

Aerin stroked her hand along his lean jaw, gazing into his eyes, wondering if she was a fool for thinking he was falling for her. And wasn't she an even bigger fool for falling for him? She couldn't hide from the truth any longer. She had fallen in love with him the moment he kissed her. How was that even possible? But then, hadn't so many of her clients told her similar stories about their journey to happy ever after? Even her two best friends and business partners had experienced the sudden dart of Cupid's arrow. A first glance, a first touch, a first kiss, a first date—all or any of those things had happened to other people, including her own parents and older brother.

'It will seem strange not being able to kiss you when we get back to London. I mean, we never even pecked on the cheek before. You always seemed to keep your distance. Not like I can talk. I did too.'

Drake twirled a strand of her hair around his finger, sending shivers up and down her spine. 'We might have to keep our distance for a while, to let things go back to normal.'

Normal? Normal was not healthy for her, Aerin knew that now. 'I guess…' Her teeth sank into her lower lip, her thoughts in a tangle. Her checklist flashed up in her mind and she inwardly cringed at how naïve she had been to write that stuff down. Who could ever tick every box? And just because one or even two weren't ticked, did it mean all of the others that were didn't count for something?

Drake's features were set in grave lines. 'It'd be crazy to continue this back home. We couldn't hope to keep it a secret for long.'

Aerin forced a smile of agreement to her lips. 'Of course. That's what we agreed—just this weekend.'

A frown pulled at his intelligent forehead.

'There's one other thing we haven't considered.'

'What?'

'The snow.'

'Oh...'

Drake eased himself away from her and rose from the bed. She couldn't take her eyes off his naked form as he strode to the windows. Her hands had caressed almost every inch of his body. How could she go back to London and pretend this hadn't happened? Her body was so tinglingly aware of him. Of his every movement. His every glance in her direction. She would have her work cut out for her, disguising her reaction to him in future. Every nerve in her body tingled when he was near her. The sensual energy he stirred in her was not something she could so easily switch off.

Aerin slipped on her wrap and padded over to join him by the window. Not only had the snow not melted, more was falling in soft, silent flurries. 'It's so beautiful...' She couldn't disguise the sense of wonder in her voice.

Drake placed his hand on the small of her back. It was such a light touch and yet it sent a warm wave of longing straight to her core. He was still looking out at the view, his forehead creased in a frown. 'Yes, it is. Thank God it's not a blizzard, though.' He turned to face her, his hand moving from her lower back to settle on her hip. 'We might have to stay a couple of extra days. Is that going to be a problem for you and your work?'

Another couple of days...snowbound with Drake Cawthorn.

It was a problem, but not in the way he probably thought. It could snow for a month, two or three even and she would be happy here with him. Shut off from the rest of the world in their own little bubble of physical bliss.

'It's not a busy time for us just now, so it will be okay. I do have a wedding the weekend after next, though. But what about you?'

He gave a shrug of one broad shoulder. 'I'll get my secretary to reschedule my commitments.'

There was a beat or two of silence.

Drake glanced at her mouth and his hand on her hip gently nudged her closer to his body. A delicious shudder went through her as his other hand cupped the back of her head. 'I'm aware that if I hadn't brought you here away from the reunion hotel, you wouldn't be stuck here with me now.'

Aerin lifted her hand to his face and stroked the jagged scar on his left eyebrow with her finger. 'I don't feel stuck with you, in fact, quite the opposite. I feel free in a way I've never felt before.' Her finger came down to trace around his mouth. 'I didn't realise making love could be so…so amazing. I mean, I've talked to friends and so on, but I didn't realise the sheer power of it. The way it takes over your body and your mind and makes you feel so euphoric.' She lowered her hand to place it back on his chest. 'I'm glad I got to experience it first with you.'

Drake captured her hand and held it up to his mouth, within kissing reach of her fingertips, his eyes holding hers. 'I sensed you were uncomfortable pretending to be in love with me in front of your friends. I thought it'd be easier to be up here on our own.' His mouth twisted along rueful lines. 'But then I couldn't stop myself from wanting you.'

Oh, the irony.

Aerin had hated lying to her school friends, she had hated the thought of being caught out and found to be an imposter. But had she truly been pretending to be in love with Drake? Or had the real thing, the real emotion hit her the first time he kissed her? It certainly felt like it. Something had happened as soon as his mouth pressed against hers. Something she had no words to explain other than it was almost other-worldly. A magical sense of rightness that his mouth was the first to kiss hers.

Aerin leaned into his embrace, her free hand going up to play with his thick dark hair. 'I couldn't stop myself wanting you either. You're rather hard to resist when you kiss me so thoroughly.'

His eyes glinted and he drew her closer to the hot, hard heat of his body. 'Is that a hint to kiss you again?'

She gave him a coy smile. 'Only if you want to kiss me.'

He brought his mouth down to just above hers. 'I do.'

Some hours later, Drake was lingering over a second coffee in the kitchen while Aerin examined the contents of the pantry and fridge in order to plan dinner in a few hours' time. They had had a snatch-and-grab breakfast, which had been closer to lunch-time after they had made love.

Made love.

It was weird but he was finding it hard to think of having sex with Aerin as anything but making love. His many previous encounters were only ever about sex. The physical release of temporary passion. Satisfying to a point but not in any other way than physically. But with Aerin, he found it difficult to keep his emotions separate. Knowing he was her first lover was part of it. He was woke enough not to view a woman's virginity as a prize or trophy or even a gift on her part to bestow. But knowing he was her first, that she had chosen him, trusted him to make love to her, was an experience he knew he would not forget in a hurry.

'There's enough food here for a week or two at least,' Aerin said, closing the pantry door.

'Let's hope we don't have to be here that long.' Drake knew he should have chosen his words more carefully by the crestfallen look that came over her features. He put his cup down and went over to her, running his hand down the length of her spine. 'I'm sorry, I didn't mean it the way it sounded.'

Aerin lifted her gaze to his, a wounded look still shimmering in hers. 'It's okay...'

Drake cradled her face in both of his hands. 'It's not okay if you feel hurt by something careless I've said. I like being here with you. In fact, I wish we could stay a week or two.'

'You do?'

He planted a soft kiss to her lips, then lowered his hands from her face to take possession of her hands. 'But we both have work and other commitments. And people are going to wonder where we've got to.' He gave her hands a light squeeze. 'Have you told anyone where you are?'

'No, because we're not due back in London until later tonight. But I'll have to text Harper and Ruby to tell them I won't be back at work for a couple of days at least.'

'Will they put two and two together, do you think?'

'Knowing Ruby and Harper, yes.' A worried look came into her eyes. 'I don't want to lie to them. It was hard enough with my school friends but I'm not as close to them.

Ruby and Harper are used to me carrying on about how cynical you are and how I always try to avoid you. I'm not sure I can be like that now that I know you better.'

Drake released her from his hold and went back to pick up his now cold coffee. But at least it was something to do with his hands. 'We have to go back to normal, or as normal as possible.' He put his cup down again on the table and scraped his hand through his hair. Emotions were bubbling inside him, but he was doing all he could to suppress them.

He would hurt her more if he extended their fling. He couldn't offer her any of the things she wanted for her life. But how were they ever going to go back to normal? By making love they had changed their relationship. *He* had changed their relationship and he couldn't change it back. He wanted her with an ache that was getting harder to manage each day. He was not used to the intensity of such feelings. He had never experienced anything quite like this before. In a weird way he was like Aerin—he wanted things he couldn't have. Fate had decided that for him. He was always going to be the tragic boy who lost his family through the despicable actions of his father.

He could not love again.

He would not love again.

He would not fail again.

How could he guarantee his love for someone would be enough to keep them safe?

'I guess you'll be glad to get back to your playboy life as soon as you can,' Aerin said with a hint of bitterness in her tone.

Drake wanted to tell her how, lately, he had started to hate his playboy life. He hated the shallow encounters, the short flings that didn't mean anything to either party other than physical release. He had been physically close with so many women but not one of them had unpicked the lock on his emotional fortress.

But Aerin with her kind and sweet nature had cast some sort of spell on him. A spell he could feel intensifying the longer he spent with her. He had found talking about his past painful for sure, but it had also released some bound-up darkness inside him. Freeing him in a way he had not been in years. Not totally free, but free enough for him to spread his cramped emotional limbs, to shake off the numbness, the deadness, to get the blood flowing again.

Drake came back to her and took her hands in his again. 'I will miss you, being with you like this. It's been…something special, something really special. I want you to know that.'

She swallowed and looked at him so openly and earnestly his heart spasmed. 'I'm sorry. I shouldn't have been snarky about your choice of lifestyle, it's just that I hate the thought of you missing out on what a real relationship feels like, one that is not transactional or temporary but a total commitment that lasts for ever.'

'I know you mean well, your whole working life and your personal one for that matter is about making people happy,' Drake said. 'But I've seen too many relationships fall apart, not always from lack of love, either. Sometimes it's a clash of values or the pressure of kids and illness or caring responsibilities or financial trouble. So many things can go wrong in even the best of relationships.'

Aerin gave him a sad smile. 'I know all of

that, but you have closed yourself off from ever experiencing love. I don't know how you can do it, how it's even possible to be so locked down you can't feel normal feelings. It's not healthy, surely?'

Drake lifted her chin with his finger, locking his gaze on hers. 'Don't try and fix me, Goldilocks. I'm fine the way I am.' But there was a part of him that was starting to recognise he wasn't as fine as he had once thought. His playboy lifestyle had already begun to lose its shine even before Aerin turned up at his office to ask him to be a stand-in date.

He found his work fulfilling and time-consuming but coming home to any empty house each day was not something he looked forward to as much as he had before. Being with Aerin had shown him a new way of living. It was as if a locked door in his brain had been opened just a sliver, allowing light and healing into all his dark spaces. But how could he allow the thought of letting go of the past any traction? How could he possibly hope that his relationship with Aerin would be the perfect one she was looking for? He had faced horrendous failure at fifteen. He had spent the time since avoiding it. Entering into a permanent relationship with someone, even someone as lovely as Aerin, was only going to reinforce his deepest fear—failure. Failure to love and to protect.

A defiant light came into her grey-blue eyes. 'But are you fine? You must get lonely at times. You must want more out of your relationships than a quick fling.'

'Why must I?'

Aerin caught her lower lip between her teeth, her eyes shifting from his. 'Because… never mind.' She straightened her shoulders and reset her features into a rictus smile and turned back to the pantry. 'I'm going to rustle up some dinner for us. You made breakfast and lunch…it must be my turn to do something around here.'

Drake stepped closer and placed his hands on the tops of her slim shoulders. He felt her shudder under the gentle press of his hands and heard her soft sigh. He swept her hair over one of her shoulders and leaned down to kiss the sensitive skin just below her hairline on her neck. The flowery fragrance of her hair reminded him of a cottage garden in summer, her skin was like silk against his lips. He slowly turned her to face him, her luminous eyes meeting his. How would he ever look at her in the future without wanting her? How would he return to his old life of casual one-night stands and not think of her touch, her taste, her sweet fragrance that clung to his skin and sent his senses into overdrive?

He brushed his bent knuckles down the creamy slope of her cheek in a light-as-air touch. 'I'm not interested in food right now.'

A light shone in her eyes, a spark of heat similar to the one burning deep in his body, sending flames through his blood. 'What are you interested in?'

Drake brought his mouth down to within a short distance of hers. 'I could tell you or I could show you. You choose.'

'Show me.'

He closed the distance between their mouths and lost himself in the sweet addictive taste of her. His tongue stroked for entry and she opened to him and met him with a sexy dart of her own tongue. Heat exploded in his body, making him hot and hard and hungry for more. She pressed herself closer at the same time as he gathered her tightly in his arms. He loved the feel of her slight frame against him. He loved the anticipation of making love to her, the heady build-up of tension in his body so powerful it was unlike anything he had experienced before. Her hands crept up to wind around his neck, her fingers delving into his hair, sending shivers cascading down his spine in a river of heat.

Aerin made a soft, breathless sound and he deepened the kiss, their tongues dancing and duelling and mating each other into submission. A thrill ran through him at the boldness of her desire for him. No longer shy, she stroked her hand down to the rock-hard heat of his erection, almost sending him over the edge.

'I want you.' Her voice was soft but no less demanding and it delighted him that she was growing in sexual confidence.

'Ditto,' Drake said, sliding his hands underneath the jumper she was wearing. She wasn't wearing a bra, which gave him ready access to her breasts. He bent his head and caressed the tender flesh with his lips and tongue. She responded with little gasps and groans and pushed herself against him in a silent plea for more.

He slid his hands down to her waist, holding her against the throbbing pulse of his body. 'The kitchen isn't the most comfortable place to make love,' he said. 'Let's take this upstairs.'

'I'm not sure my legs are going to get me that far after that kiss.'

'That's easily fixed.' Drake swept her up in his arms and strode towards the door.

Aerin gave a playful squeal. 'What are you doing? You'll wreck your back carrying me all the way upstairs.'

'Don't worry, I work out.'

'I know you do.' She stroked one of her hands along the bunched muscles of his arm. 'Impressive.'

They got to the bedroom a short time later and while Drake was breathing heavily it had nothing to do with carrying Aerin. Or at least not because of her weight. It was the feel of her in his arms, the warm lithe body pressed against his, knowing she wanted him as much as he wanted her. He laid her down on the bed and stood looking at her for a moment. Her hair was splayed out over the pillows in a golden cloud, her eyes were shining with anticipation, her smile like a ray of sunshine. She was wearing a jumper and leggings and he soon peeled them off her body, before stripping off his own clothes.

He got a condom from his wallet and came down beside her on the bed. She reached for him without saying a word. But what else needed to be said? The mutual desire that crackled between them had not lessened but grown in intensity.

Aerin stroked her hands down his chest to his abdomen, slowly, slowly, slowly, ramping up the tension in his body to breaking point. Her touch wreaked havoc on his self-control. Red-hot pleasure shot through his body, luring him to the abyss where the dark magic of oblivion beckoned.

Drake had to stop her taking him over the edge because he wanted to ensure her pleasure first. He drew her hand away from his body and kissed his way down from her breasts to her belly, lingering over her feminine mound, breathing in the musky scent of her body that signalled her high arousal. He used his fingers to separate her folds, then tasted the honeyed dew of her desire with his tongue. She squirmed and whimpered as he increased the rhythm of his caresses, her body bucking and arching as she orgasmed. Her cries of release made him want her all the more. Her passion was so unfettered, so unrestrained it made him wonder if she would find the same freedom to express her sexuality with someone else.

Someone else...

Drake wished he could eradicate the thought from his mind. He didn't want to think about her with anyone else. He didn't want to think of her making love with some other guy who wouldn't make her pleasure a priority. A guy who might exploit her or pressure her into doing things she wasn't comfortable doing.

Aerin let out a long shuddering sigh and reached for him again. 'Can I try something on you?'

'What?'

She gave a sultry smile and wriggled down his body. 'I want to taste you like you tasted me.'

'You don't have to. I don't want you to do anything you're not comfortable doing.'

'But I am comfortable with you.'

And Drake was comfortable with her. Way too comfortable. To the point where he was wondering how he was going to manage without her going forward. He shuddered at the thought of her mouth and tongue on his most intimate flesh. How could he say no? 'Okay. But if you don't want to go the whole way, then don't.'

But she did and of course it was mind-blowing, earth-shattering and sent him into a tailspin from which he thought he might not ever recover…

CHAPTER NINE

LATER THAT NIGHT after dinner, Aerin took the opportunity to text Ruby and Harper about not being back in time for work as planned. Harper called her instead of texting a reply.

'What's going on?'

'Nothing. We just got caught out with the weather.'

'Who's we? Are the rest of your reunion friends there too?'

Aerin bit her lip. How could she lie to one of her closest friends? Especially Harper, who had been lied to throughout her childhood by the father who abandoned her even before she was born and then failed to come to her aid when her mother died. 'You can't tell anyone but I'm here with Drake. Alone. He took me to a lovely cottage in the country because the reunion hotel room was a bit cramped. It only had one bed and no sofa. But then a weather front came over and we got snowed in. We can't leave until it melts.'

Harper whistled through her teeth. 'Way to go, sister. Snowbound with your worst enemy.'

'He's not any such thing.' Aerin knew she sounded overly defensive but couldn't strip back her tone in time.

'Well, well, well,' Harper said. 'Looks like you two have kissed and made up.'

There was a beat or two of telling silence.

'And not only kissed, if I'm any judge,' Harper said.

'I'm not saying anything because I promised Drake I wouldn't. He doesn't want our…erm, involvement to be in the gossip pages. Nor do I want my family to know.'

'Hon, are you sure you're not getting in over your head? You're a babe in the woods when it comes to men like Drake Cawthorn.'

'I know what I'm doing.'

'So, what happens when you come back home? Will your secret involvement continue?'

'No, that's the agreement. We end it as soon as we get back to London.' Her heart ached at the thought of ending their relationship. How would she handle it?

Harper sighed. 'Oh, hon. I can sense heartbreak looming.'

'You were the one who suggested I ask him to come to the reunion with me,' Aerin pointed out.

'I know and that's why I'm worried about you now. You've got the softest heart and he has the hardest. How is that ever going to work out?'

It was Aerin's turn to sigh. 'Tell me something I don't already know.'

Two days later, although the snow was still thick on the ground, the sun was out and shining, making the countryside look all the more stunningly beautiful. London seemed a long way away and Aerin dreaded returning, knowing it would spell the end of this magical time with Drake.

Drake joined her outside and squinted against the blinding bright sun. He held his hand up to shield his eyes. 'The snow won't last long with a bit of sunshine.'

'No...'

He lowered his hand from his face and

looked at her. 'This is the first time in a long time that I've taken time off work. I need to do it more often but there's always another client or a pressing court issue.'

Aerin looped her arm through his and he drew her closer to his side. 'You've always been a high achiever. Tom told me you left everyone in the shade at university.'

He gave a soft grunt. 'Yes, well, I had something to prove, I guess.' He gave her a grim smile and continued, 'I wanted my life to count for something to make up for the loss of my mother and sister. They didn't get to reach their potential, so I made sure I more than reached mine.'

Aerin leaned her head against his shoulder, wishing she could take away his pain but knowing it was impossible. How could anyone get over such a tragic loss? 'I'm sure they would be very proud of you.' She waited a beat and asked, 'What was your sister's name?'

'Natasha but I always called her Tash. My mother's name was Rosemary.'

There was a long silence before he spoke again.

'Thank you.'

'For?'

'For not asking what my father's name was. I hate remembering him in any capacity. His whole life was built on lies and deception and double-dealing. My mother was drawn in by his charm and only realised her mistake when she gave birth to me. Everything changed after that. He became even more controlling, and it only got worse when Tash was born two years later. I did all I could to protect them, but it wasn't enough. I can't tell you how many times I begged my mother to go to the police, but she was too frightened to do so. I think she knew he would kill her if she left him. I didn't understand that dynamic as a kid but I do now.'

Aerin put her arms around his waist and held him tightly. 'Oh, Drake, I can't bear the thought of all you've suffered.'

His arms gathered her closer, his chin resting on the top of her head. 'Enough talk of my awful past. Do you know what I'd like to do right now?'

'Make love?'

He gave a short laugh. 'Not here in the snow. When was the last time you made a snowman?'

'Years and years.'

'Shall we?'

Aerin smiled. 'I'd love to.'

Within minutes they had built a rather impressive-looking snowman with black stones for eyes and twigs for arms. Aerin stood back to look at their handiwork. 'We need a carrot for his nose.'

'Hold that thought.' Drake went back to the house and came out soon after with a carrot. 'Here you go. One carrot as requested.'

Aerin placed the carrot on the snowman and stood back. 'I wonder how long before he melts?'

'Who knows?' There was a strange quality to Drake's voice, and when she glanced up at him he was looking at the snowman with a frown carved deep in his forehead.

Maybe he was thinking about his own frozen state. His locked-away heart that he refused to open to love. What would it take to melt the armour around him?

And was she the one to do it?

The sunshine did its job, so when Aerin and Drake woke the next morning, the roads were clear enough for travelling back to Edinburgh. Aerin was determined not to be teary or clingy when it came time to say goodbye. Within a few hours, they had landed back in London and Drake drove her to her flat. He had been silent for most of the journey, as had she.

Drake carried her luggage up to her flat and set it inside the door. He straightened and smiled but it didn't reach his eyes, which were shadowed and shuttered. 'I guess I'd better get going.'

'Would you like a cup of tea or something?' She could have bitten her tongue off for sounding so eager to keep him with her a little longer.

A flicker of something passed over his face. 'I'd better be on my way.' He hesitated for a long moment and then reached for her, holding her in a tight hug against his tall frame. 'Take care of yourself, Goldilocks.' His voice was so husky it sounded as if he had swallowed a handful of gravel.

A choking lump formed in her throat. 'I will.'

Drake slowly released her and looked at

her upturned face for another beat or two. 'Keep sending those clients my way, okay?'

Aerin forced a smile to her lips. 'I will.'

And then he was gone.

Drake let out a breath he had been holding for what felt like years. So, that was it. Goodbye and thanks for the memories. But it was different somehow. Different because he would be seeing her again, either at her parents' or brother's house or through their work connections. He would have to put the memories of their time together in Scotland to one side. He must not think about her in that way. He must not recall the gentle touch of her hands, the sweet but explosive heat of her mouth. The warm silky welcome of her body and the earth-shattering release that powered through them both.

He shuddered and strode to his car, hunching his shoulders against the icy rain that had started. He had never once broken his vow of sobriety. Never once had he craved the taste of alcohol to numb his senses, to blank out his mind. But right then, he wished he could find a way to numb himself from the pain of saying goodbye.

'So, how was your trip?' Cathleen, his secretary, asked the following morning.

'Fine.'

She leaned back in her chair and surveyed him with an assessing look. 'First holiday you've taken in years.'

'It wasn't a holiday.'

'What was it, then?'

It was the best time I've had in for ever. I feel like a different man. I feel freer than I've felt in years.

Disturbed by his torrent of thoughts, Drake masked his features and leafed through the sheaf of papers she had prepared for him on her desk. 'I was doing a favour for a friend.'

'Aerin Drysdale, right?'

He flicked faster through the paperwork, trying not to picture Aerin's naked body in bed beside him. Trying not to remember how it felt to hold her in his arms while she came apart in pleasure. Trying to remind himself that it was dumb of him to be thinking about her at all. Their fling was over. It had to be. 'I need to catch up on a bit of work for the next couple of days. I don't want to be interrupted unless it's an emergency.'

'Okay.'

He turned for his office further down the corridor and then stopped and looked back at Cathleen. 'Could you send Ms Drysdale some flowers?'

'What will I tell the florist to write on the card?'

Drake paused to think about it but couldn't come up with anything. 'Just get them to deliver them here and I'll drop them off myself after work.'

What are you doing? You can't last a day without seeing her?

He dismissed the voice of his conscience. He wanted to check on her, to see her again, to reassure himself she was still okay with the end of their fling. He wasn't okay with it, though, and that was a problem, one he had not faced before. Would it be an option to extend their fling? To spend more time together? He weighed it up in his mind. Aerin knew he wasn't the for-ever type. She knew he wasn't the type of man who could or ever would tick all her boxes. So why not continue their fling for a little while longer?

Are you out of your mind? his conscience prodded him, with another warning, but he pushed it aside.

He was only dropping off a bunch of flowers, not going down on bended knee.

That was never going to happen.

Aerin heard Mutley barking in Mr McPhee's flat opposite. She had only seen her neighbour once since she'd got back and he hadn't looked well. She'd promised to check on him after work but he wasn't answering the doorbell. She went back to her flat to fetch the spare key he had insisted on giving her a couple of months ago. She was on her way back to open his door when she heard firm footsteps come up the stairwell. Her heart came to a shuddering halt when she saw it was Drake, carrying a huge bunch of flowers.

Under any other circumstances she would have smiled and given him a hug, but her worries about her neighbour took precedence. 'Drake, can you help me check on Mr McPhee? He's not answering the door and Mutley is barking. I'm worried something is wrong.'

'Sure.' He put the flowers inside her door and then came over and took Mr McPhee's key from her. He opened the door effortlessly and Mutley came bounding out, yapping loudly and then running back and forth as if to say, *Follow me*.

'Mr McPhee? It's Aerin… Oh, no…' She had only got as far as the sitting room when she saw the old man's slumped figure on the sofa.

Drake moved past her and squatted down beside the sofa and took one of the old man's wrists to search for a pulse. 'Call an ambulance.' His air of command somehow helped her to keep calm, well, calmer than she would have been on her own.

The ambulance was there in under five minutes and the paramedics loaded Mr McPhee onto a stretcher. Aerin filled them in on what she knew about Mr McPhee's health and she was even able to bundle up his collection of medications that he kept in the kitchen.

'Are you his daughter and son-in-law?' one of the paramedics asked.

Aerin wasn't game enough to look at Drake. 'No, I'm his neighbour and Drake is...erm...just a friend.'

'Is there someone to take care of the dog?' the other paramedic said, clearly a dog lover who recognised the distress the poor old dog was feeling with his master semi-conscious on a stretcher.

'Yes, of course, I'll do that,' Aerin said without thinking it through in any detail.

The ambulance left and Aerin let out an exhausted breath. 'Oh, Drake, I'm so glad you showed up when you did. I'm not good at emergencies. I just panic and freeze.'

His arms came around her and held her close. 'You did great. He'll be well taken care of and hopefully he'll be home soon.'

She swallowed and looked up at him. 'But what if he's not?'

Drake stroked her hair back off her face, a wry smile slanting his mouth. 'That big soft heart of yours is going to get you into trouble one day.'

It already has.

It would be so easy to say the words here and now. They were perched on the end of her tongue like a team of nervous divers, baulking at the distance they had to dive headfirst into. 'Seriously, though,' Aerin said, glancing at the woeful-looking dog at their feet. 'What am I going to do with Mutley? I work full-time and he's used to having Mr McPhee with him all day to take him out for his toilet breaks. If he barks too much, the neighbour will complain to the landlord.'

'What about a dog shelter? Or a boarding kennel?'

'No, he's too old for either of those, especially since he's always been with Mr McPhee.' She chewed at one of her fingernail cuticles, then added, 'I'd take him to my parents, but Mum's developed an allergy to dog hair.'

Mutley shuffled over and sat at Drake's feet and looked up at him imploringly, his tail sweeping the floor like a feather duster.

'He wants you to take him,' Aerin said.

Drake held up his hands like two stop signs. 'Oh, no, I'm no pet-sitter. I work long days and often stay away overnight when I'm—'

'Surely you could put your playboy life on hold for a week or two? He'd settle better at your place because you have a garden.'

Drake set his mouth in an adamant line but then Mutley whined and wagged his tail again. 'Don't look at me like that.' He growled at the dog without malice.

Aerin laughed. 'He adores you. I think he senses you're a strong leader. Dogs need that, they get nervous if they're not given reliable leadership.'

Drake let out a long ragged-sounding breath. 'I knew it was a mistake coming to see you tonight.'

'Why did you?'

'I wanted to give you some flowers.'

'In person? Why not have them delivered?'

'This is why.' He took her by the upper arms and planted a lingering kiss on her lips.

Aerin melted into his embrace, relishing in the warmth and pent-up passion in his kiss, wanting him so badly it was a hollow ache deep inside.

Some breathless moments later, she eased back to look up at him. 'I'm not sure what's going on. You said our fling had to end once we came back to London.'

Drake stroked his thumb across her lower lip, his eyes hooded. 'It didn't feel right just dropping you off last night and carrying on as if the last few days never happened.'

Aerin tried to keep her hopes in check. What was he actually offering her? 'So, are you saying you want to continue our...involvement?' She was not fond of the term 'fling' when it came to what they had shared together. Those wonderful memories of being in his arms would be tainted if she referred to it as a fling.

Drake took her hands in his. 'I'm not ready to end it.' His voice had a rough edge and his eyes looked haunted.

'But you will end it.' It was a statement, not a question. A fact written on a tablet of stone that weighed down her heart with its cruel veracity. 'Not tonight, not next week but some time soon you will end it.'

'I can only offer you a fling.'

She squeezed her eyes shut on the word. 'Please don't call what we had together a fling. It was much more than that. You know it was.'

Drake squeezed her hands as if he never wanted to let her go. 'I want more time with you.'

'How much time?'

His throat rose and fell over a tight swallow. 'I don't know. I just want more time.'

Aerin knew she should insist on a clean break then and there but what if more time together actually helped him open up even more? He had shared with her so much, things he had not shared with anyone else, not even her older brother, who was his closest friend. Didn't that count for something? Didn't that suggest that *she* could be the key to opening his heart to love? Aerin let out a wobbly breath. 'Okay, but how are we going to keep our involvement a secret?'

A flash of relief lit his gaze and he drew her closer to his body, his arms wrapping around her. 'It's no one's business but ours what is going on between us. I'd like to keep it that way for as long as possible.'

Aerin didn't like to tell him she had more or less told Harper what was going on between them. Harper would have guessed in any case, so too Ruby, but still. 'So, how are we going to do it? I mean, are we going to meet in secret or—?'

'Can you come and stay at my place for a few days?' Drake asked. 'It will help Mutley settle in to have someone familiar there.

It's closer to your work and far more private than a tenement flat.'

Aerin's eyes widened. 'Are you sure that's a good idea? I mean, do you ask many of your lovers to stay over?'

'Never, but you're different. Besides, it's only until Mr McPhee comes out of hospital. After that we can reassess.'

'How come you haven't had lovers stay over before?'

Drake's expression was shuttered. 'I've got used to living alone. I've been doing it since I was eighteen. I'm not the most convivial host but I would like you to stay.'

It wasn't a difficult choice, although it should have been given the sharp prods her conscience was giving her. Reminders about her plan for her life, the checklist she had so carefully written in order to find her Mr Perfect. Extending her temporary relationship with Drake Cawthorn was hardly going to help her achieve her goal. Not unless he morphed into the man of her dreams. But then, he already was the man of her dreams but he didn't want to be. He didn't want to be anyone's soulmate. He didn't want to love anyone with his whole heart. But the temptation to have more time with Drake, private time at his lovely home in Bloomsbury, was too much to resist.

He was too much to resist.

CHAPTER TEN

AN HOUR OR so later, Mutley was curled up asleep in his basket on Drake's sitting-room floor in front of the fireplace, snoring as if he belonged on a critical care chest ward. Drake was still wondering what the hell had come over him to agree to mind the scruffy mutt that looked like something out of an alien movie. But it just went to show how Aerin could get him to do almost anything.

Inviting her to stay with him was another thing that surprised him. He wasn't keen on visitors at the best of times. But then, Aerin was hardly a visitor. She was his current lover. For how long, he wasn't sure and that gave him a niggling sense of unease. He was usually very sure of when a fling was going to end, because he was the one who ended it.

But everything about his fling with Aerin was different.

Aerin was sitting on the sofa opposite him with a cup of hot chocolate cradled in her hands. Her slim legs were folded beneath her, her hair a golden cloud around her shoulders. 'Mutley looks quite at home.'

Drake gave a non-committal grunt and took a sip of his own hot drink before putting it on the table beside the sofa. He patted the cushion next to him. 'Why don't you come over here?'

Her eyes lit up and a shy smile curved her mouth. She put her drink down on the coffee table between the two sofas and came over to sit beside him. He laid one arm along the back of the sofa near her shoulders, his other hand picked up one of hers and he raised it to his mouth and kissed her bent knuckles. 'Have you heard how Mr McPhee is doing?'

'Not yet.' She sighed and glanced at her watch on her wrist. 'But I'm not his next of kin so they're hardly likely to tell me much. He has a son, but I don't think he's seen him in ages. I think he might live overseas. Do you think I should try and track him down?'

Drake played with the silky tresses of her hair. 'I can do that for you.'

'Oh, would you? I'd be so grateful. I have

a big wedding this weekend and I'm starting to panic about it. I'm usually so organised but, with the reunion and our extended stay in Scotland, I have some serious catching up to do.'

He curled a strand of hair around his finger. 'Where's the wedding? Somewhere local?'

'Kent, on the most beautiful estate the bride's parents own. The service is at a local church. I hope the weather is kind to them, the bride and groom are such a lovely young couple. I want everything to be perfect for them.'

'It's a tricky time of year for a wedding, I would've thought. Don't most people want a spring or summer wedding?'

'Yes, but the groom is dying of a brain tumour. There isn't time to wait for spring or summer. He might not make it to Christmas.'

Drake frowned. 'That's sad.'

'Yes, it is. But it's so wonderful to see how much they love each other. They truly are soulmates.' Her shoulders slumped on another sigh. 'I'm not sure how Yelena will cope without Viktor. He's her whole world and she is his.'

'It seems a risky business loving someone,' Drake said. 'You stand to lose them one way or the other.'

Aerin looked at him with her clear grey-blue gaze. 'Yes, but that's not a good enough reason to not love at all.'

He forced a smile and threaded his fingers through her hair again. 'Time for bed?'

'We'd better take Mutley out for a toilet break first.'

'I'll do that,' Drake said, rising from the sofa. 'You head on up.'

'Are you sure?'

'Absolutely.'

By the time Drake had taken the old dog out and waited for him to sniff the entire garden for the right place to take a leak, more than half an hour had gone by. Mutley finally waddled back in and went back to his bed in front of the fireplace. Drake offered him a treat, but the dog gave a rattling sigh and lowered his chin to the cushioned bed, giving him a doleful side-eye look.

Drake gave him a gentle scratch behind his ears. 'I know you miss him. But he'll be as good as new soon.'

The old dog blinked at him and then

sighed again as if to say: *I don't believe in miracles.*

'Yeah, I hear you, buddy. I don't believe in them either.'

Aerin was in the process of unpacking her overnight bag, shaking out her work clothes for the next day, when Drake came in. 'Thank you for looking after Mutley,' she said. 'But what will we do tomorrow when we're both at work?'

'I've already organised a pet door to be installed. My housekeeper will be here too.'

'Oh, that's great. I can't really take him with me.'

'Yes, well, I'm not sure what the magistrate would say if I turned up with him, either. I guess I could pass him off as a therapy dog.'

Aerin smiled. 'I think he'd be brilliant at it. He's such a sweet old thing.'

Drake began to unbutton his business shirt. 'Do you want a shower before bed?'

'Are you having one?'

His eyes darkened to pitch. 'Want to join me?'

She walked over to him as if programmed

like a robot to do everything he commanded. 'Sounds like fun.'

He gave a wolfish smile and peeled the clothes from her body, feasting on her naked form. Aerin stood proudly before him, thrilled at the way he found her so desirable. She set to work on his clothes, enjoying the sight of him fully aroused. He took her by the hand and led her to his luxurious bathroom. The shower was one of those open ones that was big enough for a crowd. He turned on the rainwater shower and once the water was the right temperature, they stepped under the spray.

Aerin tilted her head back, enjoying the water pressure but enjoying even more the pressure building in her body at Drake's closeness. Their wet bodies were locked together under the cascading water, the sensuality of it spine-tingling.

He kissed her firmly, passionately, desperately as if it had been years instead of hours since they last kissed. His hands glided down her wet body, stroking, caressing, stirring her senses into overdrive. He lowered his mouth to each of her breasts, then got on his knees and parted her intimate folds with his fingers, and then caressed her with his lips and tongue.

The orgasm hit her like a crashing wave, pulsing through her so violently she cried out and shook uncontrollably. Drake held her by the hips to stabilise her, the ripples and aftershocks still rumbling through her until finally they dissipated.

Drake straightened and pulled her close to his hardened form, his eyes gleaming in triumph. 'I love watching you come.'

Aerin was still trying to catch her breath. She placed her hands on his chest, stroking his rock-hard muscles and delighting in the heat and strength of him. She moved down his body as he had done to her, intent on subjecting him to the same intimate caress. She took him in her mouth and drew on him, confident now on how to pleasure him. He buckled at the knees and groaned but she kept going, emboldened by the way he was responding to her. He tensed and then spilled his essence, a low deep groan escaping from his lips and his whole body shuddering in the aftermath.

Aerin straightened and smiled at him. 'You sounded like you had a good time too.'

Drake gathered her close in a warm hug, his breathing still ragged. 'The best.'

Aerin was at work the following day with her friends Harper and Ruby. She'd had no choice but to tell them where she was currently staying because Ruby had suggested dropping by her flat that evening after work.

'You're staying with Drake Cawthorn?' Ruby's eyes almost bulged out of her head. 'But why?'

Aerin explained about Mr McPhee's stroke and Mutley needing a temporary home while Mr McPhee was in the rehabilitation centre. 'And I like being with Drake.'

'You're in love with him,' Harper said.

'Yes, I think I am.' Aerin sighed and continued, 'Strike that. I know I am.'

'How many boxes does he tick on your checklist?' Harper asked.

'Not many.'

'How many?' Ruby asked.

Aerin rose from her chair and paced the room. 'I think I made a mistake writing a checklist. I mean, how many people could tick every box? I know he's not perfect, but then nor am I. But I can't imagine life without him now. I love being with him.'

'Neither of us can tell you what to do,' Harper said. 'Ruby and I have been in your situation—in love with a man who we thought could never love us back. But I'm reluctant to say things will work out for you like they did for us because life doesn't always work out the way we want.'

'I know and I'm being careful.'

'But moving in with him?' Ruby said, frowning. 'What do your parents and brother think?'

'They don't know we're seeing each other. Anyway, I'm only staying with him until Mr McPhee comes home from rehab and can take Mutley back.'

Harper and Ruby exchanged worried looks.

'Please stop worrying about me,' Aerin said. 'I do enough of that myself. I know this is crazy. I know it but I can't help myself. I love Drake and I want to be with him.'

'Have you told him how you feel?' Harper asked.

'No.'

Ruby chewed at her lower lip. 'Are you going to at some point?'

'I don't know…maybe.'

'He'll probably end it before you get the chance,' Harper said. 'And that is going to hurt big time.'

'I know,' Aerin said on a heartfelt sigh.

Drake went on a stop-and-sniff-and-shuffle walk with Mutley after work. It was dark and cold and wet, but he had kind of got used to the old dog's company over the last week. But the thing he most looked forward to was when Aerin came in from work. He loved waking up next to her in the morning. He loved going to sleep with her in his arms at night. He loved sharing a meal with her and chatting about the days' events.

He loved…

He stopped as if he had slammed into an invisible wall. No. No. No. Love was not part of what he felt for Aerin. They were having a fling, an extended fling that was a little bit different from his usual ones. That didn't mean he was falling in love. He had no intention of falling in love with her or anyone. Ever.

Drake was only just back from walking the dog when his phone rang. He glanced at the screen and saw it was Aerin. He ignored the little jump of his heart, the tick of his blood, the thrum of excitement at hearing her voice. 'Hey, I thought you'd be home by now. Are you working late?'

'No, but I have to drop by my flat to pick up some things. I didn't bring much with me last week.'

'I'll swing by your office and take you.'

'Are you sure?'

'Of course. We can grab a bite of dinner somewhere afterwards.'

There was a little silence.

'Are you sure that's a good idea? Us being seen dining out in public?' Aerin asked. 'What if it gets back to my family?'

Drake was starting to realise the clandestine nature of their fling was a little compromising for someone as upfront and honest as Aerin. She loved her family dearly, so lying to them about her involvement with him must be hurting her. But then, her family weren't being completely honest with her either. Her brother Tom had met with him only the day before about seeking a divorce.

It wasn't something Drake was at liberty to talk to Aerin about. She had such rose-coloured glasses on when it came to relationships. It would crush her to find her brother was leaving his wife. But to Drake, it was only further confirmation that most relationships were doomed to fail one way or the other.

'They'll have to find out sooner or later,' Drake said. 'We can't hide for ever.'

'But we're not going to be together for ever, are we?'

'No, but that doesn't mean we can't go out to dinner like a normal couple.' Drake was aware of the tension in his voice and tried to take a calming breath.

There was another beat or two of silence.

'Drake, don't bother to pick me up. I think I'll stay at my flat tonight. I need some time to think about things. I'll catch up with you tomorrow.'

A pain seized him in the chest. A panicked feeling as if he was losing control of a situation he had thought was well under control. 'If that's what you want.' It wasn't what he wanted at all but he was not going to beg her to change her mind.

'It's what I need right now.'

You're what I need right now. You're everything I need.

The words were inside his mouth, but he couldn't get them past the stiff line of his lips.

'Drake?'

'Yes.' His voice was cold as the rain dripping down the back of his coat collar.

'I thought you must have hung up on me.'

'I have to go,' Drake said. 'Mutley needs his dinner.' He ruthlessly clicked off his phone and shoved it in his pocket.

Aerin slipped her phone in her tote bag, distressed by the outcome of her conversation with Drake. But equally determined to spend a night at her flat to get her thoughts together, to get some perspective. Talking to Ruby and Harper had made her realise the trap she had fallen into. She was living in hope that Drake would fall in love with her. And yes, that had worked for her friends, but it didn't mean it would work for her. She had always been an optimist, glass-half-full type of person but she was starting to see how deluded she was in thinking everything would magically work out.

Sometimes, tragically, it didn't.

The doorbell rang later that night and Aerin's heart leapt in hope. Had Drake changed his mind? Had he regretted his abrupt end to their conversation? Had he come to apologise? To beg her to come back and stay with him tonight? But when she opened the door, it was her brother, Tom, standing there. 'Tom? What are you doing here?'

'Can we talk?'

Aerin stepped back to let him in. 'Of course.' She closed the door behind him. 'Are you okay?'

He drew in a breath and released it in a staggered stream. 'I saw Drake yesterday.'

'You did? He never mentioned anything about it.'

Tom frowned. 'When did you last see him?'

Aerin only then realised her gaffe. 'Oh, erm, I run into him from time to time, you know, referring clients to him and so on.' She could feel her cheeks heating and could barely look her brother in the eye. 'How are you? How is Saskia?'

Tom rubbed a hand down his face. 'We're getting a divorce.'

Aerin stared at him as if he had just told her he was an alien from outer space. 'What?'

He compressed his lips. 'That's why I met with Drake yesterday.'

'So, you're the one instigating a divorce? But why?'

'It's not working any more. Saskia is clearly unhappy.'

'But she's had, what, two or three miscarriages? How could you expect her to be happy? It doesn't mean she doesn't love you.'

Tom's shoulders drooped and two spots of red appeared high on his cheekbones. 'I made a stupid mistake.'

Aerin's stomach dropped like a novice diver pushed off the ten-metre diving board. 'Oh, no...'

'It was dumb and crazy and I still can't explain why I did it. I had a one-night stand with a woman I know from work. It meant nothing.'

'I never thought you would cheat on

Saskia.' Anger and disappointment laced her tone in equal measure. For all of her life she had looked up to and idolised her older brother. And now she was finding he had clay feet after all. She had thought he had the perfect marriage A solid and forever marriage like her parents. The marriage she aspired to have one day. But now she was beginning to realise love wasn't always perfect. Was any relationship perfect?

'I'm sorry,' Tom said. 'I know how hard this is to hear but I wanted to tell you face to face.'

'Do Mum and Dad know?'

'Not yet. I'm going to see them this weekend. I'm not looking forward to it. I can only imagine what Dad will say. And Mum will be shattered. You know how much she loves Saskia.'

'How is Saskia?'

'Angry, hurt, disappointed.' He rubbed at his temple as if a tension headache was building.

'Has she agreed to the divorce?'

'Yes.'

'But she might change her mind. She

needs time to heal, to forgive you. To learn to trust you again.'

Tom gave a rueful twist of his mouth that was nowhere near a smile. 'I'm not sure that's going to happen any time soon.'

'Do you still love her?'

He held her gaze for a moment or two then sighed and looked away. 'Of course I do. I just lost my way for a bit. The stress of losing all those babies and not being able to make it right for her did my head in. I've been a prize jerk. I didn't think I was the sort of man who would cheat on his wife. She deserves better.'

'Oh, Tom, I wish I could wave a magic wand and make everything right for you and Saskia, but I have my own issues to work through.' She licked her dry lips and continued, 'I've been seeing Drake.'

Tom's eyebrows shot up. 'Seeing him as in...?' He left the sentence hanging.

'I asked him to my school reunion in Scotland and we kind of drifted into a fling. We've been keeping it a secret.'

'You know it won't last. He won't allow it to.'

'I know and that's what I'm working through.'

'You're in love with him.'

Aerin screwed up her face. 'Is it that obvious?'

'Have you told him?'

'No. Do you think I should?'

Tom gave her a grim look. 'I'm hardly the one to be dishing out relationship advice.'

'But you know him so well.'

'No one knows Drake well,' Tom said. 'He's always been a bit of a closed-book type of guy.'

'Good luck with Mum and Dad. I'd come with you for moral support, but I have a wedding in Kent this weekend.'

'Thanks, but this is something I have to face on my own.'

Aerin closed the door to her brother a short time later and leaned back against it with a heavy sigh. It was like a bad dream to think of Tom and Saskia breaking up. She couldn't get her head around her brother's fall from grace. It was so unlike him and yet, who knew what anyone was capable of while under extreme stress?

CHAPTER ELEVEN

DRAKE HAD TO force himself not to text or call Aerin all day the next day. As someone who enjoyed periods of solitude to reflect on things, he was the last person who should be criticising her for wanting a bit of space. But he wanted her, and it was killing him to be left hanging, not knowing if she wanted to continue their fling or not.

But when he got back from his evening walk with Mutley, he found Aerin sitting on the step outside his house.

'Why haven't you used the key I gave you?' he asked.

She rose from the step and huddled further into her coat. 'I didn't feel comfortable letting myself in.' She bent down to pet Mutley, who, unlike him, was a lot less inhibited about showing how excited he was to see her. The silly old dog yapped and wagged its tail and panted as if it were going to have a heart attack in delight.

'Let's get out of this infernal cold,' Drake growled. 'Tell me why I live in London again?'

Aerin gave a soft laugh. 'It's hard not to think about a tropical island in the sun right now, that's for sure.'

Drake could think of no one he would enjoy being with on a tropical island more than her. Maybe that would solve the problem of keeping their fling a secret. They could take a holiday to some exotic faraway location where they could relax and soak up the sun.

He led the way inside his house, and Mutley immediately shook his wet fur, sending droplets of water all over the floor. 'How's Mr McPhee doing?'

'He's progressing well,' Aerin said, shrugging off her coat. 'He's using a walker, which he hates but he realises he needs it for balance.'

'It must be hard to get old and not be able to do the things you want to do.'

'Yes…'

Drake took her coat and hung it on the

stand near the door. 'I'm sorry I ended our conversation so abruptly last night.'

'That's okay. I did kind of spring it on you about staying at my place instead of here. But just as well I did, as Tom dropped around unannounced.'

'Oh? How was he?'

'Why didn't you tell me you saw him the other day?'

Drake shrugged off his own coat and hung it next to hers. 'He saw me as a client, that's why. I don't break client confidentiality.'

'But surely you could have told me? I'm his sister and you and I are…are…in a relationship.'

Drake raised his scarred eyebrow. 'And here I was calling it a fling, silly me.' He knew his tone was mocking. He knew his expression was cynical, but he was cornered by her use of the term *relationship*. It was too…serious. Too confining. Too threatening.

Aerin pursed her lips, staring at him for a long moment without speaking. 'Is that all I am to you? Just another one of your casual lovers?'

'No, of course not.'

'Then tell me what you feel about me.'

Drake opened and closed his mouth, not sure he could find the words to describe how he felt about her. 'I care about you. You're a nice person to be around.'

'You care about me.' Her tone was jaded. 'Would you say you liked me?'

'Of course I like you.'

'What about love?'

His throat suddenly constricted. 'What about it?'

Her gaze was direct. 'Do you love me?'

Drake disguised a swallow, but it was as if he were choking on razorblades. 'Why are you asking me that? We agreed on a short-term fling. Love has nothing to do with two people enjoying a mutual attraction to each other.'

Her small chin came up to a defiant height. 'You won't say it, will you? You act like a man in love and yet you can't or won't say the words.'

Drake wanted to plug his ears like a wilful child and chant *la-la-la* so he didn't have to listen. 'And I suppose you're going to tell me you've fallen madly in love with me?'

Her eyes glittered. 'Would there be any point?'

'No.'

'Because those words frighten you. They make you uncomfortable. They make you feel vulnerable. But I'm going to say them anyway. I love you, Drake. I think I fell in love with you when you first kissed me. I didn't expect such a thing to happen. I certainly never saw you as my Mr Perfect. But I can't help feeling the way I do. I don't want to be in a fling with you. I want more than that.'

Drake raked a hand through his hair, his chest so tight he could barely draw in a breath. 'You're probably confusing good physical chemistry with something else.'

'I know my own heart. I know what I feel. Don't fob me off with it being infatuation or due to my lack of experience.'

'I'm not the settling-down type, I told you that from the get-go.'

'I know and I shouldn't have allowed things to progress the way they did but I couldn't help it. I wanted you and you wanted me and the rest, as they say, is history, or at least it is now.'

He frowned and narrowed his gaze. 'What do you mean?'

She gave him a sad smile and plucked her coat off the hook. 'It's time to say goodbye. I'm ending our relationship before any more damage is done. You're not ready for love. You have too much armour around your heart. And only you can remove it.'

Drake took a step towards her but then pulled himself into line. He had to let her go. He couldn't demand anything of her. He didn't have the right. He shoved his hands into his trouser pockets to keep them from reaching for her. 'You do realise we'll still have to see each other at times.' His voice sounded as frosty as the wintry air outside.

'I don't see why we have to.'

He pointed to the dog sitting at his feet. 'What about him?'

Aerin glanced at Mutley and then back at Drake. 'I'm sure you can deliver him to Mr McPhee some time without running into me. Text me and I'll make sure I'm not around if it makes you feel that uncomfortable.'

He thinned his lips into a cynical smile. 'So, you'd rather not see me? Fine. You won't.'

Aerin pressed her lips together. 'I think it's probably for the best. A clean break.'

She put her coat on and it took everything in him not to help her with it as he usually would. But he knew if his hands touched her again, he would not be able to let her go.

He held the door open for her instead. 'Can I give you a lift?' He wasn't that much of a bastard to let her find her way home alone.

'My car is up the street.'

'I'll walk you to it.'

'There's no need.'

'Indulge me.'

She gave a sigh of resignation. 'Okay.'

They walked along the street until they came to her car. Drake opened her driver's door for her and waited until she had clipped on her seat belt before closing it. He stepped back on the pavement and walked back to his house without even waving goodbye.

Aerin was in a final meeting with Ruby and Harper before the wedding in Kent that weekend, so told them of her decision to end things with Drake.

'Oh, hon,' Harper said, giving her a hug.

'I know how hurt and miserable you must be feeling. I wish I could say it will all work out in the end but that's not how life pans out sometimes.'

'It's so heartbreaking for you,' Ruby said, also enveloping her in a hug. 'But you've only been in a fling with him for a short time. Maybe he's not sure of his feelings yet.'

Aerin stepped out of Ruby's embrace and painted on a brave smile. 'Thanks for your support. It's hard but I'm determined to get through it. The hardest thing will be watching him go back to his playboy lifestyle. It's going to really sting to see him out and about with someone else.'

'Yes, of course that's going to be tough to face,' Harper said. 'But hopefully, you'll soon find your Mr Perfect and your time with Drake will be just a distant memory.'

Aerin had a feeling she would not forget about her time with Drake in a hurry. And she had an even bigger feeling that her notion of a Mr Perfect waiting out there for her might be a fantasy she needed to let go of and fast.

Drake called in to see Mr McPhee a few days later at the rehabilitation centre. He had planned to bring Mutley in with him for a visit but when he rang the centre, they said it was against their policy to allow pets in. He had only been in Mr McPhee's room a few minutes when he realised the centre was not the place he would send any of his relatives to—if he had any. The old man was clearly miserable, and the meal that was congealing on a tray was not fit for a stray dog, let alone an elderly person who needed good nutrition to get back on his feet.

'How are you doing?' Drake asked.

'Not so bad.' Mr McPhee tried to smile but couldn't quite pull it off. 'How's my wee laddie, eh? Aerin told me you're doing a grand job of taking care of him for me.'

'It's no bother at all,' Drake said, realising with a jolt it was true. He enjoyed the old mutt's company, especially now that Aerin had ended their fling. And the walks morning and evening, stop-start as they were, did take his mind off things…a bit. 'But he misses you. And I bet you're missing him.'

'I am…' Mr McPhee sighed and looked away.

'Has your son been in yet?' Drake had managed to track down Mr McPhee's son, but he got the sense the son was not all that interested in visiting his old and frail father.

'Yes, but he can't get here for a wee bit. He's a busy man. Runs his own company in Spain.'

In his work as a lawyer, Drake had met too many relatives like Mr McPhee's son. People who were too busy to take any interest in their elderly relatives' welfare while they were still alive but who were the first to phone to ask when the estate was being finalised once they had passed away.

'Have you seen Aerin?' He was annoyed at himself for asking but he was so desperate for news of her. He was acting like a lovesick fool but he couldn't seem to help it.

'She came in yesterday on her way to a wedding in Kent, bless her.'

Drake licked his suddenly dry lips. What had Aerin told the old man about their relationship?

Mr McPhee must have sensed his discomfiture and said, 'She put me straight on your relationship, that you're just friends.'

Drake was worried they might not even be that now. 'I'm not what she's looking for.'

Mr McPhee eyeballed him. 'Why do you think that?'

'Has she talked about her checklist?'

'Och, aye, it's not a bad idea in today's world to know what you want and then go and look for it. My Maisie was the same, so organised and always knew what she wanted.' He gave a soft chuckle and then his gaze became wistful. 'I wasn't in with a chance at the beginning, to tell you the truth. I had a lot to learn but I worked hard and won her over in the end. I learned that you don't find your soulmate, you become one.'

You don't find your soulmate, you become one.

The words were so profound, so wise and insightful, Drake wanted to jot them down in his notes folder in his phone so he wouldn't forget them. Maybe he had a lot to learn too. Maybe it was time for a bit of self-reflection about his attitude to relationships. He knew it stemmed from his tragic past. But how could he move past it?

'You must miss her terribly,' Drake said.

'Oh, I do,' the old man sighed. 'But I could have lost her so much earlier by not changing in order to win her over. I'd never told anyone I loved them until Maisie. Then I told her every day we were married, and those three words were the last words she heard before she took her last breath.'

I could have lost her so much earlier by not changing...

But Drake had lost Aerin. He had lost her by not recognising what he felt for her. The feelings that had grown from the moment he'd kissed her, but he had tried to squash, to ignore, to crush. Feelings that had sprouted and grown inside him regardless, nurtured by the sunshine of her smile, the healing magic of her touch. He'd been too afraid to speak his feelings out loud.

But he wasn't afraid now. The old man's wise words had triggered a realisation that he only had one life and what would that life look like without love? Without Aerin? A sad and lonely empty life. His father had destroyed Drake's family but why should he allow his father to destroy his ability to love? Not all love was toxic. Not all love failed. Not all love was perfect, but it was love, and he realised now he couldn't live without it. He could not escape the tragic end that came to his mother and sister, but he could escape the emotional prison his father's actions had placed him in.

Life was worth living to the full. Loving was part of being fully human. There was no guarantee he wouldn't end up sad and lonely as an elderly widower. He thought about the bravery of the young couple marrying this weekend in Kent, the courage of the young bride, Yelena, marrying her sweetheart, Viktor, even though he hadn't long to live. Drake was a fool to fail to grab life with both hands now and enjoy everything loving someone with your whole heart offered.

Drake put his hand on Mr McPhee's shoulder. 'I'm going to have you transferred to somewhere nicer than this. Somewhere you can have Mutley with you for part of the day. How does that sound?'

The old man's eyes watered. 'It sounds expensive. I don't have the money for anything like that. I'm fine here. Don't worry. I'll make do.'

Drake took one of the old man's craggy hands in both of his. 'I owe you for making me see what I couldn't see before. I love Aerin like you loved your Maisie. I'm going to tell her now, even though I'll be gate-crashing a wedding to do it.'

Mr McPhee beamed. 'That's my lad, you go for it. I'll be cheering for you all the way.'

Aerin stood at the back of the church as the young bride and groom exchanged their vows. It was sad and poignant and happy at the same time. The groom was in a wheel-chair, too frail to walk, but the bride stood proudly beside him and promised to love him in sickness and health, till death do us part. Harper was doing the photography and Aerin could see her every now and again brushing at her eyes before she took the next shot. Her assistant running the video was also having trouble holding back tears. Jack was in the back pew, bouncing Marli on his knee, not far from where Aerin was sitting. Ruby and Lucas were further along, hold-ing hands, the love they felt for each other plain for all to see.

It wasn't often that the wedding plan-ner and caterer and photographer's part-ners were invited to their clients' wedding, but Yelena and Viktor had insisted on them being there. Of course Aerin didn't have a partner, and it was particularly sad to be sitting, once more, on her own. Maybe it would have been better if she had been brave enough to attend her school reunion on her own and then she wouldn't have this gnawing pain of emptiness and loss.

But then she wouldn't have experienced the magic of falling in love with Drake.

Aerin heard someone come in the church behind her pew, where she was seated on the end of the row. And then a familiar deep voice asked in a gentle whisper, 'Is there room for me next to you?'

Aerin glanced up in shock to see Drake standing there. Her heart banged in her chest as loudly as the church bells had done outside earlier. What was he doing here? Dared she hope he had come to see her? No, she dared not hope. She had learned her lesson by now. She had to be sensible and level-headed about Drake Cawthorn.

'Of course.' She shuffled along, her pulse suddenly racing. 'I thought you weren't a fan of weddings?' she said softly so no one else could hear. A musical piece was being played by the wedding couple's friend, so it offered a quick moment to find out why he was here.

Drake gave a mock shudder and smiled at her. 'I'll have to get used to them.'

'Why's that?'

'Because how else will I marry you?'

Aerin stared at him with wide eyes, her heart skipping, her mouth dropping open. 'Are you...*proposing*?' She said the word as if it was the most unthinkable thing he would ever bring himself to do. Because, for the last few days, that was exactly what she had accepted. He didn't love her. He didn't want her to be with him for ever.

His dark eyes twinkled and he leaned closer to speak against her ear. 'I love you and I want you to be my wife. I couldn't wait until later to ask you. I'm sorry about gate-crashing the wedding but I couldn't waste another minute without you.'

Aerin was overjoyed, but she was forced to restrain herself due to the wedding service, which was resuming now the musical performance was coming to a close. So many feelings bubbled up inside her she could barely keep still. She was about as restless as little Marli, who was babbling and bouncing on her daddy's knee further along the row. 'I love you too. So very much. And yes, I will marry you.'

Drake pressed a brief kiss to her lips and then took her left hand and laid it on his thigh. He stroked her bare ring finger, his touch gentle, almost reverent. 'I've come without a ring. I thought we could choose one together.'

'I think that would be a lovely thing to do.'

'I also wrote a poem on my way here, given that was, what, number six or seven on your checklist?'

Aerin tried but failed to suppress a giggle, but no one seemed to notice. 'Number seven. Six is: *must have a pet or want one.*'

'Does Mutley count? I've grown quite fond of him, even if he leaves hair everywhere and farts a lot.'

Aerin smiled. 'So, what's your poem?'

'Roses are red, violets are blue, I want you in my life, as my loving wife, so please say "I do".'

'I do.'

The wedding service finally ended and Drake took Aerin's hand and led her outside to the watery sunshine. 'You've made me the happiest of men. I didn't think I could ever be happy again, not after what happened when I was fifteen. But you've made me want more out of my life. I can't live in fear of loss any more. Everybody has to face it at some point. Look at this brave young couple. They'll have to face it sooner than most and yet they've just demonstrated their love for each other.'

'Oh, Drake…' Aerin hugged him so tightly she was sure she would either break her arms or crack his ribs. 'I love you so much. I was so shocked to see you come into the church. I thought I must be dreaming. It's like all my wishes and dreams have come true.'

He brought her left hand up to his lips and kissed the back of her hand. 'My darling Aerin, I'm not Mr Perfect but I'll work on it so I can become him.'

'You're just right as you are.'

He grinned. 'Said like a true Goldilocks.'

EPILOGUE

Christmas, one year later

DRAKE PUT THE last present under the Christmas tree at Aerin's family's house in Buckinghamshire. It was a huge tree, beautifully decorated with baubles and tinsel, and twinkling LED lights. The whole family was gathered, and he was now a bona fide part of that family. It gave him a true sense of belonging he had never felt before. Or maybe it was because he was happy in himself, happy with the man he had become rather than the man he had been. How could he have lived in that emotionless prison for all that time? He would still be in it if not for his beautiful Aerin.

Aerin came up beside him and looped her arm through one of his. 'Isn't it wonderful that Mr McPhee could join us?' Her eyes shone with happiness. 'He's over there chatting to my dad with a whisky in his hand. And Mutley has made himself quite at home near the fire.'

Drake glanced at the old dog, lying on his side, snoring contentedly in front of the roaring fire in the hearth. He had become increasingly close to Hamish McPhee over the past year. Hamish had become the father figure he had longed for all his life, a reliable, well-regulated elder who was wise in his counsel and fun to be around as well. 'I'm glad they both made it this far. I had my doubts there for a while.'

'You saved them both by moving Mr McPhee to the private rehab centre. He never looked back after that. He's even walking without the walker now.'

Drake was pleased with the old man's progress, but he was also pleased with his own. He had had to be rehabilitated into recognising and articulating his feelings. And he had worked at not being so worried about loss. He was preparing for the loss of both Mutley and Mr McPhee, knowing there were some miracles you could not pull off. But young Viktor, the groom from the wedding at Kent last year, was still miraculously with his adoring wife Yelena. A new treatment had become available—hideously expensive, but Drake was happy to donate to such a good cause and it had worked so far. It had bought them some time, and that was surely another thing to celebrate at this time of year.

There had been another happy ending in that Tom and Saskia had decided to work at their relationship rather than to press on with the divorce. They were now back together and expecting a baby in the spring.

Speaking of babies, Harper and Jack were expecting another baby, a boy this time, due in a matter of days. Their other celebration was the success of Jack's first watercolour exhibition, which was a sell-out. Jack had put his dream of being an artist on hold when his father died, in order to take over the running of the family hotel business. But it was with Harper's love and encouragement that he finally got to pursue his love of painting.

Ruby and Lucas had exciting news too— they were expecting a baby. So far the gender was still a secret but Drake knew they would be fabulous parents. It was an experience he was looking forward to in the not so distant future. He had never wanted to be a father until he fell in love with Aerin. She would be the most wonderful mother and he looked forward to raising a family with her. He was confident that their little family would feel secure in his love and protection, unlike the example his own father had set.

Drake took Aerin's left hand where not only a beautiful diamond ring sat but a wedding ring as well. They had married before her thirtieth birthday in January and it had been a fabulous celebration. Only a wedding planner with Aerin's skill set could have organised a fabulous wedding so quickly. It was a day he would never forget as long as he lived. Seeing her walk up the aisle towards him had been the most amazing experience. One that made his heart overflow with love and hope for a long and happy future together.

'Happy, my love?' he asked.

'So happy my heart feels like it is going to burst.'

Drake drew her closer, his own heart feeling so full it was taking up all the room in his chest. 'I wrote you another poem. Want to hear it?'

Her eyes danced. 'Yes, please.'

'I love you as the ocean loves the shore, I love you as the wind loves the autumn leaves, I love you as far and wide as the sky, I love the life we have together, the future as yet unknown. But I love that we can face any weather or any season because we are each other's own.'

'Oh, darling that was perfect!'

'Perfect, eh?' Drake grinned. 'That's what you are, my love. Perfect in every possible way.'

* * * * *